As Of Glory Carson Would Be His Wife, And He Would Be Her Husband.

He had two weeks to observe her in that role and decide if she was a viable wife candidate.

He also had only two weeks to convince Glory that having a husband around the house wasn't a rotten way to live.

Bram yawned. The thing was, the two weeks had to have an aura of authenticity to them. Bringing home flowers and candy every night wasn't realistic.

The best way to handle this was just to be himself, do what felt natural and right.

Yep, Bram concluded, as sleep edged over his senses, he'd just be Bram Bishop, the man, come Monday evening.

No...he'd be Bram Bishop, the *husband*.

Dear Reader,

This month we have some special treats in store for you, beginning with *Nobody's Princess,* another terrific MAN OF THE MONTH from award-winning writer Jennifer Greene. Our heroine believes she's just another run-of-the-mill kind of gal…but naturally our hero knows better. And he sets out to prove to her that he is her handsome prince…and she is his princess!

Joan Elliott Pickart's irresistible Bishop brothers are back in *Texas Glory,* the next installment of her FAMILY MEN series. And Amy Fetzer brings us her first contemporary romance, a romantic romp concerning parenthood—with a twist—in *Anybody's Dad.* Peggy Moreland's heroes are always something special, as you'll see in *A Little Texas Two-Step,* the latest in her TROUBLE IN TEXAS series.

And if you're looking for fun and frolic—and a high dose of sensuality—don't miss Patty Salier's latest, *The Honeymoon House.* If emotional and dramatic is more your cup of tea, then you'll love Kelly Jamison's *Unexpected Father.*

As always, there is something for everyone here at Silhouette Desire, where you'll find the very best contemporary romance.

Enjoy!

Lucia Macro

Senior Editor

Please address questions and book requests to:
Silhouette Reader Service
U.S.: 3010 Walden Ave., P.O. Box 1325, Buffalo, NY 14269
Canadian: P.O. Box 609, Fort Erie, Ont. L2A 5X3

JOAN
ELLIOTT PICKART
TEXAS GLORY

SILHOUETTE *Desire*®
Published by Silhouette Books
America's Publisher of Contemporary Romance

For Pam Vallentine

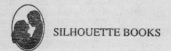 SILHOUETTE BOOKS

ISBN 0-373-76088-4

TEXAS GLORY

JOAN ELLIOTT PICKART

is the author of over seventy novels. When she isn't writing, she enjoys watching football, knitting, reading, gardening and attending craft shows on the town square. Joan has three all-grown-up daughters and a fantastic little grandson. In September of 1995, Joan traveled to China to adopt her fourth daughter, Autumn. Joan and Autumn have settled into their cozy cottage in a charming small town in the high pine country of Arizona.

Welcome to Texas,
home of perpetual matchmaker Granny Bee...and her latest project:
the Bishop Boys, confirmed bachelors turned...

FAMILY MEN

Margaret Madison m. ?
TEXAS BABY
Special Edition
Winter 1997
That's My Baby!

Tux m. Nancy Shatner
TEXAS MOON
Desire #1051, 2/97
Man of the Month

Blue m. Amy Madison
TEXAS DAWN
Special Edition #1100, 5/97

Bram m. Glory Carson
TEXAS GLORY
Desire #1088, 8/97

LEGEND:

—— The Bishop brothers and respective wives

- - - - Maternal relationship between Margaret Madison and daughter Amy

Prologue

"Tell you a story? Why, I'd be mighty pleased to do just that. I'm figurin' you want to hear 'bout Bram Bishop. So make yourself real comfy there, and your ol' Granny Bee will tell you all 'bout Bram.

"Now, you know that two of the Bishop boys up and got themselves married. Tux is with his Nancy. Blue is with his Amy. They're happy as can be.

"Bram was mighty pleased that his brothers found the forever love they were seekin'. But, oh, mercy, Bram surely did wish himself a fairy godmother with a magic wand, who would produce a lovin' lady for *him* to marry. He just wasn't havin' any luck findin' a wife, none at all.

"Well, one day Bram was gettin' on an aeroplane to fly back to Houston, after doin' some business over Austin way. I never been on an aeroplane and don't intend to, either. I'm just fine right here in my ol' rockin' chair.

"Anyway, that plane had three seats glued together on each side of the aisle. Can you imagine that? There wasn't even room for a person to put their knittin' bag 'longside their chair 'cause they're stuck plum together.

"You got a little piece of paper tellin' you what seat you're to settle yourself in. Silly business, if you ask me. But Bram was lookin' for the seat number on his special paper, 'long with the other folks all shufflin' in a row on that plane. Bram found his place and saw a lady already in the seat by the window.

"Now, that's where my story really begins, you see, with that pretty little gal by the window. Glory be, she was... Funny I should say that word...Glory..."

One

Glory Carson leaned her head back and closed her eyes, telling herself to tune out the noise of the other passengers boarding the airplane.

Good grief, she thought, she was so exhausted she was nearly numb. The seminar in Austin for psychologists specializing in marriage counseling had been well attended, resulting in a constant cacophony of jarring voices. She'd had to be her professional best at all times, a constant smile in place, her interest in who was speaking to her at least appearing to be at the maximum.

It had been a productive weekend...she hoped. She'd pressed her business card into more hands than she could count, and been promised a half dozen referrals. All she could do now was wait and see if they materialized in her office.

Her speech had been well received, Glory mused foggily. The applause had been loud and long, and afterward the favorable comments were numerous.

All in all, she had no complaints about the way things had transpired in Austin, except for the fact that she was so tired she practically had to remind herself to inhale, then exhale.

Oh, what she would give for a bubble bath, then bed, and hours and hours of undisturbed, rejuvenating sleep.

Glory was vaguely aware of activity next to her, but she kept her eyes closed, assuming the passenger in the middle seat was settling in.

Fine, she thought. The sooner everyone got their bottoms planted, the quicker this plane could leave Austin and make the hour flight to Houston and home, and her waiting, welcoming bed.

"Where's your seat belt?" a man with a rich, deep voice asked. "Oh, here it is. There you go, buddy. You're all set. You sit there and behave like a good little guy. Okay? See? I'm right here next to you."

Oh, dear, Glory thought, apparently she had been seated next to a father with a young son. She adored children, she really did, but she hoped to the heavens that this one was well behaved and *quiet*.

Moments later, as the airplane began to move, Glory allowed the rumble of the engines to drift over her senses like a comforting blanket. She was semiconscious of the pressure of liftoff, the plane tilting, then straightening again.

She was up among the peaceful clouds, she thought

dreamily. It was a perfect place for a nap.

Glory gave way to blissful slumber.

Bram Bishop leaned slightly forward to get a better view of the woman in the seat next to the window.

Sleeping Beauty, he thought, just like in the fairy tale. Man, oh, man, she was one beautiful woman.

Her strawberry blond hair was swept away from her face to clearly display her delicate features. He couldn't tell if her hair was just extremely short or if she had one of those bun gizmos.

Long lashes fanned her peaches-and-cream cheeks, and her lips were slightly parted, begging to be kissed.

The silky, rose-colored blouse she was wearing defined lush breasts, and her navy blue slacks gave evidence of gently sloping hips and long legs.

And there was no wedding ring on the third finger of her left hand.

"Want to trade seats?" Bram said to the traveling companion he'd boarded the plane with. Certainly not expecting a reply to his question, Bram frowned, grabbed a magazine from the pocket in front of him and settled back in his seat.

His lousy luck was running true to form, he thought. He was in close proximity to a gorgeous lady, and she was sound asleep! She was a captive audience for getting-to-know-you chit-chat during the hour flight, but was she smiling, eager to communicate? Hell, no.

Bram shook his head in frustration, flipped through the magazine, then jammed it back into place.

He was beginning to believe that he'd never find a wife, a woman to share his life, have their children, be the other half of his dream of forever love. He'd begun his quest to find the woman of his heart more months ago than he cared to count.

The decision to marry had been a mutually agreed-upon project with his brothers. Both Tux and Blue had done it, the lucky sons-of-guns. Tux had Nancy. Blue had Amy. They were couples. Husbands and wives.

And he, Bram Bishop, was still alone and, damn it, lonely, with no one even in the running as a candidate for his wife.

What was wrong with him? He was a nice guy, decent looking, and he had a prosperous construction company that was growing by leaps and bounds. He liked babies and puppies and had learned, at his mother's knee, which fork to use and the importance of treating women with gentlemanly respect at all times.

When he was part of the swinging singles scene, he'd had women falling all over him. But ever since he'd decided he wanted to get married, that flock of females left a lot to be desired.

Bram sighed.

Well, he'd just have to hang in there, not give up, stay ever alert for a possible wife candidate. It sure as hell would help his cause, though, if pretty women like the one seated by the window would stay awake long enough for him to at least say hello.

Bram glanced up to see the flight attendant making her way slowly down the aisle. She was pushing a cart and distributing drinks and small packages of peanuts to the passengers.

Well now, he thought, opportunity was knocking. Sleeping Beauty was going to miss out on having a refreshing beverage if she continued to snooze.

The considerate thing for him to do would be to gently wake her and inquire if she was thirsty. She could always go back to sleep if she wasn't interested in either a drink or in talking to him.

Good plan.

Except...

How did a man rouse a sleeping woman he didn't know? What part of her delectable person should he touch to ensure she wouldn't start hollering for the cops?

Bram unsnapped his seat belt and leaned forward to get a full view of the woman. Reaching across his companion in the middle seat, Bram tentatively pressed one fingertip on the lady's knee.

Glory raised her lashes slowly, reluctantly, unaware she was turning her head to the side at the same time.

In the next instant her eyes flew wide open, and she stiffened. A scream began to build in her chest and work its way up to her throat, headed for her mouth.

She was staring at the biggest, stuffed toy panda she had ever seen.

"Oh, Lord," Bram said, watching the reactions of the woman.

Without thinking it through, Bram clamped his hand over the woman's mouth. She shifted her terrified eyes to his face.

"Don't scream," Bram whispered. "Please, stay calm. I just thought you might want a cool drink. The flight attendant will be here in a couple of minutes. I didn't mean to frighten you. Okay? Are you with me here?"

Flight attendant? Glory's mind echoed frantically. Oh, yes, of course, the airplane, the flight home to Houston. Fine. She understood now.

What wasn't fine, though, was that a strange man, albeit an incredibly handsome man, had his large hand over her mouth. Also not dandy was the fact that there was an enormous toy panda, with seat belt in place around its fat middle, sitting next to her.

Glory frowned. Bram removed his hand quickly from her mouth and produced his very best smile.

"Hi," he said, "I'm Bram Bishop. I'm really sorry I startled you. I guess I should have let you sleep through refreshment time."

Wrong, he thought. Sleeping Beauty awake was even more beautiful than Sleeping Beauty asleep. She had the most expressive green eyes he'd ever seen. They completed her lovely features to perfection.

"And you are?" Bram said pleasantly, raising his eyebrows.

"Not happy," she said, glaring at him. "You scared me half to death. You can't go around poking a woman's knee. You're going to end up in jail one of these days."

"Oh," he said. "I really am sorry. I was trying to be a nice guy. You know, didn't want you to miss having a drink if you wanted one."

"Mmm," Glory said. She looked at the panda. "And what, or who, is that?"

Bram straightened slightly, patted the bear on the head and chuckled.

"Great bear, huh?" he said. "See, I was in Austin on business and my brother, Tux, telephoned me. Tux is a year older than I am. I have a twin brother named Blue, too. Blue and Amy were married last month.

"Anyway, Tux married Nancy about a year ago, and they just found out they're going to have a baby. Tux was so excited he decided not to wait until I got home to tell me the big news.

"I read an article once that said newborn babies can decipher black and white from the time they're born. So, when I saw the panda I knew it was the perfect gift for my niece or nephew.

"Of course, this is the middle of May and the baby isn't due until Christmas but—" Bram shrugged "—it's a terrific panda. Don't you think so?"

Glory blinked, trying to digest all that Bram Bishop had said.

"You...you bought the panda a ticket on this flight?" she asked finally.

"Well, yeah," Bram said, nodding. "I figured it would get really messed up if I sent it through with my luggage. Since it's nearly five feet tall, it was too big for the overhead compartments, so I bought it a ticket for a seat of its own. Hey, this is a very important bear for a very special baby."

"Right," Glory said, eyeing him warily. "Well, one thing is clear. The baby is going to have an interesting uncle—to say the least."

Before Bram could decide if he'd just been insulted, the flight attendant arrived with her offerings. Bram asked for a soft drink. Glory requested orange juice.

"Would your friend like anything?" the flight attendant asked Bram. She had a perfectly serious ex-

pression on her face as she nodded toward the panda.
"A drink? Some peanuts?"

"No, thanks," Bram said. "He gets airsick if he
eats or drinks during a flight."

"Okeydokey," the attendant said, then pushed the
cart forward.

"The craziness is catching," Glory muttered.

"I heard that," Bram said, laughing.

Heavens, Glory thought, taking a sip of her juice,
Bram Bishop had such a rich, rumbly, masculine
laugh, that it had sent a shiver down her spine. He
really was *very* good-looking. His features were rugged and tanned, his medium brown hair was sun
streaked to nearly blond in places. And he had, without a doubt, the most beautiful, bluest eyes she'd ever
seen.

Oh, yes, Bram Bishop was drop-dead gorgeous.

He was also nuttier than a fruitcake.

He'd bought a plane ticket for a five-foot toy panda
bear? Said bear being a gift for a baby who wasn't
due to be born until the end of the year?

That was definitely crazy.

Well, it was sweet, too, in all fairness. Bram Bishop
and his brothers must be extremely fond of each other.
That was nice. A close-knit family certainly wasn't a
given in today's society.

"So!" Bram said, interrupting Glory's thoughts.
"I've introduced myself and my buddy here. It's your
turn. You are…?"

"Glory Carson," she said, smiling.

Say, now, Bram thought, what a lovely smile Glory

Carson had. It lit up her whole face and made those fascinating green eyes sparkle.

"That's a pretty name," he said. "Glory. I really like it."

"Thank you."

"So tell me, Ms. Glory Carson—it is *Ms.*, isn't it?"

"I'm not married," she said.

She could, she supposed, correct Bram, tell him she was actually *Dr.* Carson, but she wasn't in the mood to go into a lengthy explanation about her work, not after the weekend she'd just put in. She was having an hour's flight worth of time-out.

"I'm single, too," Bram said, then drained his cup. "That's one thing we have in common already."

Already? That was a red-alert word, Glory thought. Mr. Bram Bishop just might be starting his hustle, making his move, his come-on. Oh, this malarkey got so tiresome.

"That didn't sound right," Bram said, frowning. "My mouth got ahead of my mind. That 'already' was really tacky."

"Oh," Glory said, surprise evident on her face.

Bram smiled. "That doesn't mean I wouldn't like to get to know you better—talk, share, discover who you are. But I'm not assuming anything here."

"That's very refreshing," Glory said, unable to keep from smiling.

"Let's take it from the top," Bram said. "Do you live in Houston?"

"Yes."

Dynamite. "That's good," Bram said, nodding.

"Next question. How long is your hair when it's falling free?"

Glory frowned and finished her orange juice.

"Cancel *refreshing*," she said. "What's next? The spiel about wanting to see my hair spread out on your bed pillow? You need some new material, Mr. Bishop." She leaned back and closed her eyes. "Talk to your panda bear."

No wonder he wasn't married, Bram thought in self-disgust. He was an idiot. The thing was, he didn't have any "material," because he'd never needed it with women. He just said what was honestly on his mind. And since he was wondering how long Glory Carson's hair was, he'd asked her.

Bram looked at the panda. "I blew it, buddy."

"Indeed," Glory said, not opening her eyes.

"Cups, please," the flight attendant said, appearing next to Bram's seat. "We'll be landing in Houston very soon."

Bram reached over and plucked the cup from Glory's hand.

"There you go, darlin'," he said to the attendant. "Listen, let me ask you something."

"Yes, sir?"

"If a man you just met asked you how long your hair was when it wasn't piled on your head, what would you do?"

"Slug him," the flight attendant said.

"Thanks for sharing," Bram said glumly.

"Glad to help," the attendant said, moving on.

Glory had to quickly smother a bubble of laughter. This really wasn't funny, she told herself. Her merriment was probably the product of her bone-deep fatigue. But Bram had sounded like a dejected little boy who'd been told it wasn't polite to ask for candy that hadn't been offered to him.

He was an unusual man, this Bram Bishop. She'd expect someone with his looks and build to be smooth as molasses around women, having them fall all over him after one glimpse of that dazzling smile, that body and those gorgeous blue eyes.

Yet he seemed to be doing everything wrong, saying the worst things possible in a first-meeting scenario.

Wait a minute, Glory thought. The key word was *seemed*. It could very well be that Bram had perfected an aw-shucks-poor-me-I-screwed-up routine that resulted in women forgiving him a multitude of social sins.

Oh, forget it. She didn't have time for this nonsense. She'd be very glad when the plane landed and Bram exited with his silly panda.

Glory opened one eye just enough to look at the toy bear.

Then again, she mused, she had to give Bram credit for doing such a sweet—though ridiculous—thing as getting that toy for his brother's baby-to-be, and actually buying an airplane ticket for the enormous bear so nothing would happen to it.

Stop it, she told herself, closing her eye again. Why was she wasting her precious time attempting to analyze the enigmatic Mr. Bishop? Enough was enough.

Glory directed her mind to go as blank as a television screen when the Off button was pushed. No matter how little time remained until the plane landed in Houston, every minute spent in a relaxed, nonthinking mode was beneficial for replenishing her energy supply.

Three minutes later she opened her eyes.

Darn it, she thought, she was becoming more tense by the second. She could no longer ignore the presence of the huge panda, *or* the man who had plunked it next to her.

She was just so *aware* of Bram Bishop sitting beyond the enormous toy. It was as though he was emanating a masculine current that crackled and hummed over and around her.

She somehow knew that he was sliding glances her way, scrutinizing her from head to toe. She could *feel* the heat radiating from Bram's gorgeous blue eyes as his gaze touched her body, causing her skin to first tingle, then draw the warmth inward, deep and low.

Nothing like this had ever happened to her before. But then again, she reasoned, she couldn't remember ever being quite this exhausted. Of course. That had to be the answer to her overreaction to Bram's blatant male sexuality. Her state of total fatigue.

But even though there was a reasonable explanation for her being flustered by Mr. Bishop, it was still disconcerting and definitely unacceptable.

Well, there was only one solution. Bram couldn't sneak little peeks at her body if she was talking to him. She could keep those compelling, dangerous eyes of his centered on her face if she chatted with him.

"So, Bram, what do you do in Houston?" Glory asked pleasantly.

Bram jerked in his seat at the sudden sound of Glory's voice.

"When?" Bram asked, just as pleasantly.

Glory frowned. "When?"

"Yeah, you know, are you asking what I do for a living during the day? Or—" his voice seemed to drop an octave "—what I do at night in my private time? What hours exactly are you interested in?"

This had not been a good idea, Glory thought. Talking to Bram was *not* solving the problem of the strange heat swirling through her. He'd taken an ordinary what-do-you-think-of-the-weather type question and somehow turned it into a sensuous image-evoking event....

Bram Bishop at night, in a room glowing with candlelight. Tall, ruggedly handsome Bram, reaching out those powerful arms to draw a woman close and... A woman? Oh, why not.... Go for it, Glory. Bram pulling *her* into his embrace, pinning her in place with those blue, blue eyes, then slowly, tantalizingly lowering his head toward her lips and...

"Glory?"

"Who?" Glory blinked. "What?" She sighed. "Never mind. I'm really too tired for chit-chat, I guess. I apologize if I've been rude in any way, Bram. I'm not at my best, by any means. I'm going to shut up until we land. It was nice meeting you. Goodbye."

"I own Bishop Construction," Bram said quickly. "Would you like me to build you a house?" He smiled. "A patio? How about a gazebo? You strike me as the type of lady who would really enjoy a gazebo."

"I do? I don't think... No, I know, I've never sat in a gazebo."

"Why not?"

"Well, I haven't had the opportunity or the time, I guess."

"Ms. Glory Carson, you should correct that as soon as possible." Bram nodded decisively. "You're definitely a gazebo person.

"Hey, don't misunderstand me here. This isn't a sales pitch to have you hire me to build you a gazebo. I simply picture you really liking one.

"Let's see now," Bram went on. "You'd wear a summer dress, one of those filmy, swishy things, and a wide-brimmed hat. Yes, that's good. Don't forget the hat. And—" he grinned "—your hair would be down, loose. Yep, that's you, all right."

It certainly was not, Glory thought. The verbal picture Bram was painting was of a woman with idle hours, who was whimsical and romantic. That definitely was *not* who Dr. Glory Carson was.

"Well," she said, "if I ever decide to have a gazebo built, I'll give you a call."

"Speaking of calling," Bram said, "I was wondering if you'd be comfortable giving me your telephone number so I could—"

"Ladies and gentlemen," the flight attendant said, "we'll be landing in Houston in five minutes. Please be certain that your seat belts..."

Damn, Bram thought, tuning out the remainder of the attendant's message. Glory had retreated behind the panda, was checking her seat belt and fiddling with her purse. There was a briefcase under the seat in front of her. Cripe, he hadn't even found out what she did for a living.

Why had she been in Austin? What had she been doing to become so exhausted? Where did she live in Houston? What was her telephone number?

Who was Glory Carson?

If his brothers knew how badly he'd blown the opportunity to gather information about a possible wife candidate, they'd razz him from now until next Tuesday.

Well, all was not lost.

They still had to land, exit the plane and walk up the tunnel. Before he was separated from Glory in the crunch of people in the terminal, he was definitely going to find out how to contact her.

He had no intention of losing track of her, because he had *every* intention of seeing Ms. Glory Carson again.

Two

Bram sank onto the sofa in his living room and muttered a word his mother would never have allowed to be spoken under her roof.

It was totally unbelievable, he mentally fumed, reflecting on the mayhem that had arisen the moment the powers that be had given permission for the passengers of the airplane to leave their seats.

He'd leaned over to retrieve the panda *and* to tell Glory Carson that he wished to speak to her—his intention being the request of her telephone number—when a little old lady, who looked no bigger than an elf, had asked him if he'd please retrieve her parcel from the overhead compartment, dear boy?

Two more women tagged him for the same job, as well as one short, stocky man. When he'd finally been able to return to his seat, the panda was still there, grinning like an idiot, but Glory was gone.

His last hope had been the luggage claim area, but no Glory Carson appeared to snatch a suitcase from the rotating jumble of luggage. Apparently she had been in Austin for a short enough stay to have a carry-on in the overhead compartment like the rest of the world.

"Damn it," Bram said, then lunged to his feet. "The telephone book!"

Twenty minutes later, Bram smacked the large book shut and glowered into space.

Nothing, he thought, shaking his head in disgust. He'd looked up every spelling of Carson imaginable. He'd even called directory assistance and come up empty. The operator had found a *Dr.* G. Carson, but Bram hadn't bothered to ask for the number.

No, Glory wasn't a doctor, for Pete's sake. They'd covered the Ms. versus Mrs. bit on the plane. If Glory was a doctor, she would have said so at the time.

Bram began to pace, the large living room accommodating his long, heavy strides back and forth across the chocolate-colored carpeting.

He'd decorated his apartment on the fifteenth floor of a high-rise in earth tones: brown, oatmeal, yellow, burnt orange and deep green. The knickknacks and pictures were of a Southwestern motif, the furniture oversize to allow for his height. The color scheme, he'd told his mother, represented Texas, which was exactly the way he wanted it.

He'd decided years before that even though he owned a construction company, he wouldn't build himself a house until he was ready to marry and settle down. Then he would draw up plans with his wife's input to create a home, not just a structure with the label of "home."

But here he was, thirty-three years old, *more* than ready to find the woman of his dreams, have babies with her, build that special home.

Here he was, alone and lonely.

And he'd let a very viable wife candidate in the form of Ms. Glory Carson slip through his fingers.

"Man," Bram said, halting his trek and dragging one hand through his hair, "this is frustrating as hell."

He spun around and started toward the kitchen, realizing suddenly that he was hungry. As he passed the panda where it was perched in an easy chair, Bram glared at the toy.

"Knock off the smile, pal," he said. "This is not a happy situation."

In the kitchen Bram began to yank food from the refrigerator, shoving all and everything onto the nearest counter.

Tomorrow, he decided, he'd talk to Tux, who was a private investigator. After Tux finished laughing himself silly over Bram's inability to obtain a telephone number from a woman held captive on an airplane, he would hopefully agree to use his investigative resources to track down Glory for Bram.

Whatever it takes, Bram vowed, as he pitched a moldy tomato into the trash. Yes, sir, he'd pull out all the stops, leave no stone unturned, and a whole slew of other clichés.

He would find Glory Carson.

*   *   *

Glory sank into bed with an exhausted sigh, savoring the feel of the marshmallow-soft pillow beneath her head.

Sleep at last, she thought. She'd unpacked her carry-on, eaten a light dinner, sorted through the maze of papers in her briefcase, checked with her answering service for messages, then finally indulged in a long, leisurely bubble bath.

And now she was anticipating hours of blissful sleep before the alarm clock shrilled the announcement that it was Monday morning and the beginning of a new and busy week.

As she began to drift off into slumber, sudden images of a six-foot-tall panda began to dance before her mental vision.

Glory's last conscious thought before sleep claimed her was that the human-size panda toy had gorgeous, sapphire blue eyes.

The next morning the panda sat in a chair in the corner of Tux Bishop's office. The huge toy now had a billed Houston Oilers cap balanced on top of its head. No respectable panda, one of Tux's investigators had declared, would be seen without a cap announcing loyalty to the city's football team.

Bram paced heavily back and forth across his brother's office, finishing his tale of having found, then lost, Glory Carson.

"It wasn't my fault, of course," Bram said, slouching onto a chair opposite Tux's desk.

"Of course not," Tux said, then paused. "Whose fault is it?"

"Our mother's. Mrs. Jana-John Bishop."

Tux chuckled. "This ought to be good. What does our sweet mother have to do with the fact that you screwed up royally on that airplane?"

"She taught us to be polite gentlemen, you dolt. What was I supposed to do when those little old ladies asked me to get their junk out of the overhead compartments? Tell them to go find a Boy Scout? Tux, Glory has vanished. I need your help here."

"Hmm." Tux rested his elbows on the arms of the chair, made a steeple of his hands and tapped his fingertips against his lips as he stared into space.

There was a definite family resemblance among the Bishop brothers, each having nicely muscled physiques on six-foot frames, rugged, handsome features, and the same deep blue eyes.

Tux's hair, however, was very blond, streaked nearly white-blond by the sun in places. Bram's twin brother, Blue, had hair as black as midnight.

"You got absolutely nothing from the directory assistance operator?" Tux said finally.

"Nope. Isn't that strange? If Glory had an unlisted number, the telephone operator would have said so. The only G. Carson was some doctor, but I know that isn't Glory."

Bram stiffened in his chair.

"Do you suppose Glory gave me a phony name?" he said. "Why would she do that?"

Tux shrugged. "According to you, she's a very beautiful woman. Maybe she gets rid of hustlers like you by inventing a name, making it impossible for you to bother her.''

''I'm not a hustler!'' Bram frowned. ''Well, I was in my former swinging single life...sort of. But not now. I'm sincere, honest and trustworthy.''

''Brave, courageous and bold,'' Tux added.

''Would you knock it off? Come on, Tux. You're the private investigator in the family, so investigate, for Pete's sake. Find Glory Carson for me.''

''Chill, little brother,'' Tux said. ''I'm leaping into action.''

''It's about time,'' Bram muttered.

Tux opened the bottom drawer of his desk and removed the telephone book, placing it in front of him.

''Oh, man,'' Bram said, ''are you deaf? I already did that bit.''

Tux glared at Bram.

''Did you check the yellow pages?'' Tux asked.

''What for?'' Bram said, flinging out his arms. ''Glory didn't strike me as someone who might be a plumber or exterminator.''

''Bishop, shut up a minute, will you?'' Tux said.

''I'm taking my bear back,'' Bram said. ''You're worthless, Bishop.''

''You can't have the panda,'' Tux said, flipping to the yellow section of the telephone book. He began to turn pages, one at a time. ''It now belongs to my son or daughter. Whew. Can you believe it, Bram? I'm going to be an honest-to-goodness father.''

Bram smiled. ''It's wonderful, it really is. You'll be a great daddy, Tux, and Incredibly Beautiful Nancy sure will be a super mother. I'm really happy for you guys."

"Thanks. We're on Cloud Nine, that's for sure. Well, actually, Nancy kind of came down off the cloud this morning when she was tossing her cookies. Morning sickness is really the pits."

"Yeah, I bet it is. What did you do for her?"

"I suggested it might be a good idea to put something back in her stomach, you know what I mean? I offered to heat up the leftover pizza we had last night."

"And you lived to tell about it?" Bram asked, raising his eyebrows.

"Just barely. I won't do *that* again, believe me." Tux leaned closer to the telephone book. "Man, I'm a top-notch investigator. I should receive an award for solving this case so quickly. Maybe I'll settle for sending you a megabucks bill."

"Why? What?" Bram said, getting to his feet.

"It's right here," Tux said, tapping the page. "Dr. Glory Carson is a psychologist specializing in marriage counseling. She has an office in a building about six blocks from here."

Bram sank back onto the chair, an incredulous expression on his face.

"She *is* Dr. G. Carson?" he said. "Why didn't she correct me when I called her 'Ms'? A marriage counselor?" He raked both hands through his hair. "Oh, hell, that's terrible."

"Why? What's wrong with her profession? Hey, it says the lady has brains, as well as looks. Dr. Carson is not a bubblehead."

"I realize that, Tux, but, cripe, a marriage counselor? She spends her days listening to people with messed-up marriages, then suggests appropriate behavior, right?"

"I guess so."

"Don't you get it?" Bram said. "This is not an ordinary woman. This is someone with an indelible ink blueprint of how things should be done in a relationship."

"Oh," Tux said. "I see your point. Well, maybe she has an open mind regarding her personal life."

"Then why isn't she married? No, she's a tough case. You should have seen the wall clank into place when I asked her how long her hair was when she didn't have it pulled back."

"You asked her that? The first time you talk to the woman, you ask her that? On an airplane? Bram, you're hopeless. You're doomed."

"I wanted to know," Bram yelled.

"It wasn't the appropriate time or place, dumbbell."

"Ah-ha!" Bram said, pointing one finger in the air. "See? There's that word again. My blunders are going to be magnified tenfold by someone whose profession is centered on *appropriate* behavior."

"Yep," Tux said, nodding slowly. "I do believe you're right, which is unusual for you."

"This is going to call for finesse, expertise, a very carefully thought through approach."

"That leaves you out. Forget Glory Carson."

"Not a chance." Bram got to his feet, reached

across the desk and tore the page from the telephone
book.

"Hey!" Tux said.

"I need this. Thanks, Tux. Hug Nancy for me.
Don't forget to feed the panda. He likes hamburgers
and fries, no mustard, extra catsup. See ya."

Tux watched his brother stride from the room, then
turned to look at the bear.

"Count your blessings that you're going to live with
me, Nancy and our baby, kiddo," he said to the panda.

Friday at noon, Glory sat at the desk in her office,
eating the lunch she'd packed at home. She usually
studied the files of her afternoon clients during the
break, but today she found she couldn't concentrate.

The week since she'd returned from the seminar in
Austin had seemed especially long, the days dragging
by. She'd recuperated energywise after a solid night's
sleep on Sunday, had typed the notes from the con-
ference into a semblance of order and placed them into
appropriate files in the cabinet.

Glory sighed.

What she had *not* managed to do during the week
was to follow her own firm directives to put Bram
Bishop out of her mind.

For some unknown and *very* annoying reason, Bram
had hovered in her mind's eye, the image so clear she
could actually hear his rich voice and rumbly laughter.

She'd purposely scooted into the aisle of the airplane as quickly as possible when she'd seen that
Bram was busy helping passengers retrieve their pos-
sessions from the overhead compartments.

While she'd chalked up her disconcerting feminine reaction to Bram's masculine magnetism as bone-weary fatigue, she was still shaken, still felt vulnerable.

She had removed herself from Bram's presence on the plane, knowing with relief she'd never see him again.

Ha, she thought dismally. Never see Bram Bishop again? That wasn't quite how the week had gone. The man and his silly panda had followed her into her dreams at night, causing her to toss and turn.

It was so ridiculous. Bram was just a man. Well, okay, he was the best-looking male specimen she'd ever encountered in her twenty-seven years, but that was beside the point.

Also of no importance was the masculine aura that emanated from Bram, the blatant male sexuality, the crackling whatever-it-was that had woven over, around and within her with disturbing, heated intensity.

Glory covered the unfinished fruit salad with a plastic lid, replaced it in an insulated bag beneath her desk, then got to her feet and roamed restlessly around the office.

As if the strange week she'd just spent wasn't bad enough, she fumed, she still had this afternoon to get through.

Each morning her secretary, Margot, placed the files of the day's appointments on Glory's desk. So what had she discovered at nine o'clock?

Bram Bishop had an appointment to see her at one, right after the lunch break.

Why?

Why would Bram make an appointment with a marriage counselor?

How had he even discovered where she was? She had *not* told him what she did for a living, nor corrected his use of Ms. to Dr.

Bram had somehow tracked her down, and in less than fifteen minutes he would be walking into her office.

What on earth did he want?

"Calm down, Glory Carson," she told herself aloud. "You're acting like an idiot."

She marched into the small bathroom off the office, freshened her lipstick and smoothed back her hair. Her fingertips lingered on the figure-eight bun at the back of her head.

How long is your hair when it's falling free?

Bram's words spoken on the airplane echoed in Glory's head, and she glared at her image in the mirror.

"Would you stop it?" she said to her reflection.

With a cluck of self-disgust, she left the bathroom and returned to her desk, placing Bram's empty file squarely in front of her.

When Bram arrived, Margot would request that he fill out a new-client form, which the secretary would give to Glory when Bram was escorted from the reception area into the office.

At the moment, however, the file was devoid of paper, and was devoid of answers as to why Bram had made an appointment to see her.

Maybe, she thought suddenly, he'd lied when he'd said he wasn't married. Maybe he was having problems in his marriage because he flirted with women other than his wife. Women, for example, who he encountered on airplanes. Maybe he needed professional help to be able to be faithful to his wedding vows.

Bram Bishop married? Yes, that was a definite possibility and would certainly explain why he wished to see her in her professional arena.

What didn't make sense was why the thought of Bram being in a committed relationship was extremely depressing.

Glory pressed her fingertips to her temples where a stress headache was beginning to throb.

Bram Bishop was driving her crazy, right out of her mind.

She narrowed her eyes.

Actually, now that she thought about it, she was glad Bram was coming to the office today. Because she was no longer in a state of exhaustion, she'd be able to view Bram in a normal light.

Yes, he was handsome, but so were a multitude of other men. Yes, he had beautiful blue eyes, but so did millions of other men. Yes, he had a nice physique, a dazzling smile, a sexy laugh, but big deal. He was just a man—no more, no less. And now Bram Bishop was just a client—no more, no less.

Thank goodness, Glory thought, she'd gotten all that straightened out. She was under control, calm, cool and collected.

The telephone on her desk buzzed.

And she'd straightened out just in the nick of time, she mentally tacked on.

Glory lifted the receiver at the same moment she

pressed the button with the blinking light in the row at the base of the telephone.

"Yes, Margot?" she said.

"Mr. Bishop is here for his appointment."

Tell him I went home, Glory's mind yelled. Tell him I died. Tell him... Glory, get a grip.

"Show him in, please, Margot."

Glory replaced the receiver, drew a steadying breath, then got to her feet. She came around the side of her desk, as she did when she greeted all clients upon their arrival.

Bram was just a man, she mentally repeated. No more, no less.

The door to the office opened and Margot stepped back to allow Bram to enter.

Wrong, Glory thought frantically. Bram Bishop was more—much more—than any man she'd previously met. Her fully rested state was doing nothing to diminish the sensual impact he was having on her as he walked slowly toward her.

He was so tall, with shoulders so wide. His features were even more rugged, tanned and compelling than she remembered. He was wearing a white Western shirt and crisp jeans that were obviously quite new.

And those eyes...dear heaven, those gorgeous blue eyes of Bram's were holding her immobile. Was she breathing? Oh, she hoped so. She'd be mortified if she fainted dead-out-on-her-nose from being in close proximity to Bram Bishop.

"Glory?" Margot said.

"Hmm?" Glory turned her head to look at her secretary, then blinked. "Oh, thank you." She took the paper Margot was extending toward her.

Margot stared at Glory questioningly for a long moment, then hurried across the room, closing the door behind her as she left.

"Well, we meet again," Glory said, sitting down gratefully in the chair behind her desk.

Her legs were trembling, she realized. Her heart was racing. There was heat—pulsing heat—thrumming low in her body. This was absurd, ridiculous and absolutely unacceptable.

"Have a seat, Mr. Bishop."

"Bram," he said, settling in one of the chairs opposite her desk. "After all, we're already acquainted, Dr. Carson. You might have corrected my use of Ms., you know."

"It didn't seem important at the time," she said. "I'll need a minute to look over this new-client form you've filled out."

"That's fine," Bram said.

There she is, Bram thought, looking intently at Glory. Man, he was glad to see her. He'd been really rattled when he discovered he'd lost track of her. But now he'd found her again, and she was even lovelier than the image he'd been carrying in his mind.

She was dressed very much as she'd been on the airplane. Ultrabusiness—cream-colored slacks, a pale blue blouse and a navy blue blazer.

What would Glory look like in jeans and a T-shirt?

And, oh, man, what would Glory look like with her hair falling free?

"You didn't answer any of the questions on the

form, Bram," Glory said, "beyond name, address, telephone number and age. There's a whole section here on how long you've been married and so forth."

Bram propped one ankle on his opposite knee.

"I told you on the plane that I wasn't married," he said, no readable expression on his face.

Glory slipped the paper into Bram's file, then folded her hands on top.

"Yes, so you said. But I thought since you'd made an appointment to consult with a marriage counselor that perhaps you actually *were* married."

"No."

Hooray! Glory thought. No, forget it. Glory, just stop it. Get it together. Professional conduct at all times, remember?

"I'm *planning* on getting married," Bram said.

"Oh, I see," Glory said. "Well, that's nice." No, that was terrible, just awful, really depressing, and... Oh, Glory, please stop. "Congratulations." She cleared her throat. "When's the big day?"

Bram shrugged. "I have no idea. Soon, I hope."

"So! What brings you here?"

You, Bram thought. But Glory had been more relaxed, more open, on the plane. In her professional setting, she was stiff as a board, her smiled forced and phony.

If he marched around the desk, hauled her into his arms and kissed her senseless, would she loosen up? No, she'd probably deck him.

Easy does it, Bishop, he told himself. Take it slow and easy.

"Well, here's my theory," Bram thought. "If a person consults a marriage counselor *before* he gets married, he stands a better chance of not gumming up the works *after* he's married. Get it?"

Glory frowned slightly. "Well, I... Well, the idea has merit, I suppose. I've never done any prenuptial counseling, but... Don't you think your fiancée should take part with you in these proposed sessions?"

A slow smile broke across Bram's face, widening into a grin.

"I don't have a fiancée," he said.

"I beg your pardon?"

"I want to get married. I fully intend to get married," he said, his smile fading. "I just haven't been able to find the right woman yet. In the meantime, I'm going to prepare myself to get married, sort of like boot camp. You know what I mean?

"I have a lot to learn about the appropriate behavior for being a husband, partner, the half of a whole. When I marry, it will be until death parts me from my wife. The Bishop boys believe in forever love." He paused. "Yes, forever love."

Oh, no, Glory thought, was that the ache of tears she was feeling in her throat? Yes, it was. Control. She had to gain control of her emotions. *Right now.*

But, dear heaven, what Bram said had been so touching, so honest and real. The words had obviously come straight from his heart, spoken in a voice low and reverent, with an echo of wistfulness.

Forever love.

What a beautiful way to express it, to define the essence of his hopes and dreams. Bram wasn't strutting his machismo stuff at the moment, he was simply being a man, rendering himself vulnerable to her censure.

Bram Bishop was asking for her help as a professional, who had expertise in an area where he admittedly was lacking in knowledge.

How could she, in all good conscience, refuse his heartfelt request?

Three

Bram was hardly breathing as he watched the changing emotions on Glory's face.

She was, he knew, weighing and measuring, reaching a decision regarding his "boot camp for marriage" theory. Personally, he considered the idea nothing short of brilliant.

Of course, his mental patting himself on the back was due to his having concocted a plan whereby he could see a great deal of Glory and really get to know her, the person, the woman.

He certainly didn't need a training course on how to be a proper husband. All a man had to do was love his wife with his entire heart, mind and soul, be faithful, be honest. That was marriage, pure and simple.

But he didn't mind *pretending* he needed training if

it accomplished his goal of discovering whether or not Glory Carson was a viable wife candidate.

Glory sure was doing some heavy-duty thinking. Come on, sweetheart, Bram silently directed, open your pretty mouth and say yes to the plan.

"Well," Glory said finally.

Bram dropped his booted foot to the floor and sat up straighter in the chair.

"Let me be very candid with you, Bram," Glory said. "I moved to Houston from Chicago about seven months ago to escape the brutal winters. I'm in the process of building my practice here, which takes time and energy.

"I've been attending workshops, seminars and giving lectures—all and everything necessary to become known in the psychologist community."

Bram nodded.

"Your idea of prenuptial counseling," Glory went on, "just might offer something different, unique and, therefore, bring in new clients."

"Oh, absolutely."

"I was wondering, though, if the concept should be offered in group sessions."

"No," Bram said, nearly yelling.

Glory jerked in surprise at his outburst.

"Sorry," he said. "But no, that's not a good suggestion. The whole thing is too personal, too private. I mean, cripe, Glory, do you think I want a bunch of strangers knowing that I'm worried I won't know how to be a good husband? A man has his pride to protect."

"Oh," she said, frowning. "Yes, of course. You're right."

Man, he was on a roll, Bram thought smugly. He could hardly wait to tell Tux and Blue about this genius-level performance.

"So you'd prefer to meet with me privately?" Glory said.

"You bet."

"Well, over the years research has shown there are ten major causes for divorce. The studies list them in the order of frequency. What if we had ten sessions together here in my office and thoroughly covered that list?"

"No."

"No? Why not?"

"Glory, look," Bram said, leaning forward and resting his elbows on his knees. "Yes, I think we should cover whatever is on that list, but there's more to marriage than we can deal with sitting in this office."

"What do you mean?"

"For example, a guy on one of my construction crews just separated from his wife. Why? Because he's an outdoors man who likes to camp, hunt, fish. His wife's idea of a vacation is a fancy hotel, shopping and going to the theater. It may not sound like a big deal, but it's blowing them apart now, even though they were aware of it before they were married."

"And?" Glory said.

"Another guy I know is miserable. He loves his wife, he really does, but they're in trouble after being married four months. When they were dating, he took her out a lot, wined and dined and courted her. Now he wants quiet evenings at home. She's still into going out at night.''

"What's your point, Bram?''

"I want to do this right, Glory, which means boot camp extends beyond the walls of this office. It's one thing to talk about potential red-alert areas, it's quite another to actually live them.''

Glory frowned. "What are you suggesting?''

"We pretend we're married.''

"What!'' she said, definitely yelling.

Bram raised both hands quickly. "Don't stress. Hear me out. Okay?''

"Oh, I wouldn't miss this for the world,'' Glory said dryly. "This is absurd.''

"It is not! I'm not saying our role-playing would include the lovemaking part of marriage. I have my principles, you know, Dr. Carson.''

Glory narrowed her eyes. "Do tell.''

"I'm trying to. We'd spend every evening together for a while, just as though we were coming together at the end of our workday like a married couple. That's important, don't you see? It's not like dating…being at one's best at all times. This would be the real goods, totally realistic.

"Glory, wouldn't you, as a professional marriage counselor, gain valuable insight into the nitty-gritty details that rip people apart? Be able to show them how to head trouble off at the pass? Wouldn't you have a much better handle on how to help couples than you do now just sitting behind that desk?''

"I'm an excellent counselor, Mr. Bishop.''

"Oh, hey, I believe it, but by doing this project with me you'd be even better. We'd both benefit. I'd learn how to be an appropriately behaved husband, and you'd sharpen your professional skills, which would surely increase your client list." Bram shrugged. "Then we go our separate ways, and that's that."

Glory stared at Bram, her mind racing.

Yes? No? she thought. From a professional standpoint, the idea had very exciting possibilities. The hands-on experiences would be invaluable, exactly as Bram stated.

But from a personal angle? Going home to Bram Bishop at the end of each workday, having dinner, spending the evening together—that scenario shouted danger in big, bold letters. There was no denying the sensual impact Bram had on her. To place herself in such close proximity to the man night after night wasn't wise, not at all.

But then again, what a marvelous opportunity to gather information that might very well benefit so many of her future clients.

On the other hand...

"Oh, drat," Glory said, pressing her fingertips to her temples, "this is crazy. I'm chasing my own thoughts around in an endless circle."

"There's really no reason to stress," Bram said. "This is definitely a win-win situation. We each accomplish our individual goals by doing something together. It's very simple, Glory."

"At the risk of sounding like an old movie," she said, "would this every-evening togetherness be at your place or mine?"

Bram shrugged. "We'll alternate. All we have to do is pretend we're home, no matter whose place it is. Do you have an apartment or a house?"

"A cottage."

Bram grinned. "With a gazebo?"

"No," she said, matching his smile. "There's no gazebo."

"That's a shame. I still say you're the type of lady who should have a gazebo."

"Ah, yes, and a filmy summer dress and a big hat to wear while sitting in said gazebo."

"Hey, you remembered what I said." Bram's smile grew even bigger.

"Well, there aren't that many fanciful thoughts in that particular compartment of my brain."

Bram's smile disappeared as he looked directly into Glory's green eyes.

"Well, I think we'll just have to do something about that," he said.

"Oh, well, I…" Glory started, then stopped, having totally forgotten what she was about to say.

Those eyes, she thought. Dear heaven, those blue eyes of Bram's were like a beautiful sea, beckoning to her to forget everything and just fling herself into their fathomless depths.

Her heart was racing, its wild tempo echoing in her ears. She couldn't move. She couldn't think. She was held in a sensuous web by Bram Bishop's mesmerizing eyes.

A quiet buzzing noise came from a small black box attached to the side of Glory's telephone. She tore her gaze from Bram's, took a quick but deep breath, then cleared her throat.

"That's the signal from Margot that our time is up," she said, looking above Bram's left shoulder.

Man, Bram thought, jerking himself back to reality. He'd lost track of where he was as he'd stared into Glory's emerald eyes. The heat low in his body was coiled, so hot, twisting.

This woman was tying him in knots, and he had a feeling she wasn't even aware of the effect she had on him—and probably on a whole helluva lot of other men who crossed her path.

There was an innocent aura surrounding Glory, as though her womanliness was asleep, her compelling femininity slumbering, not known even to herself.

She was strictly business in her tailored clothes and severe hairstyle. Her smiles were rare commodities, not easily given.

He'd dubbed her Sleeping Beauty when he'd first seen her on the airplane. That name was more appropriate than he'd even realized at the time.

"Bram?" Glory said.

"What? Oh." He got to his feet. "Right. Listen, we need to talk more about this idea of mine. Why don't we go out for a hamburger tonight and discuss the plan?"

"No, I don't think—"

"Come on, Glory. There's a lot of potential to this proposal. You said yourself you're trying to build up your practice. It won't cost you anything to discuss it further over a hamburger. Seven o'clock?"

Glory sighed. "Yes, all right."

"Great. What's your address. I'll pick you up."

Glory wrote the information on a slip of paper and extended it toward Bram.

"Better include your telephone number," he said. "You know, in case I get a flat tire on the way, or whatever, and I'm delayed."

Glory added the number and Bram took the paper.

Smooth, Bishop, he told himself. Very smooth.

"Why didn't the operator show this number as unlisted?" he said.

"It's under Carson Glory. I prefer that my clients go through my answering service, using my office number. Some people feel I should be available to them twenty-four hours a day. I'd appreciate it if you didn't give that number to anyone."

"It's safe with me."

But was *she* safe with Bram? Glory wondered. Oh, she wouldn't be in any physical jeopardy by allowing him to enter her home that evening. No, the danger stemmed from within herself, from the new, strange and unsettling reactions she continually had when close to Bram.

"I'm outta here," Bram said. "Oh, it's casual tonight, remember." He was really looking forward to seeing Glory in a pair of jeans. "Seven o'clock."

Glory stood. "Yes, fine. Goodbye, Bram."

Bram smiled, nodded, then strode from the room, leaving the door open as he left the office. Glory sank back onto her chair.

A few minutes later Margot entered. In her early sixties, short and slender, she was a widow who had six grandchildren.

"You're free until four o'clock, Glory," she said. "My, that Bram Bishop is a handsome man, isn't he? You know, the only problem with your professional specialty is that all the men you meet are married."

Glory fiddled with a pen, not meeting Margot's eyes.

"Bram isn't married," Glory said. "He...he presented a plan for a type of prenuptial counseling."

"Oh?"

"Bram *intends* to marry when he finds the right woman. He feels it would be beneficial to him to learn more about being in a committed relationship. He pointed out that if I added prenuptial training to my practice, I might build up my client list."

"You don't say," Margot said, beaming. "Well, my goodness, isn't that a marvelous idea? I assume you agreed to his proposal?"

"No, not exactly. There wasn't time to fully discuss it. We're covering the remaining details this evening, then I'll make my decision."

Margot's eyebrows shot up. "You're going out with Bram Bishop? Write that down. This is the very first date you've had since I came to work for you when you arrived in Houston."

"It's not a date," Glory said, looking up at her secretary. "It's a business dinner."

"Mmm," Margot said, still smiling to beat the band. "Keep me posted on this, Glory." She turned and hurried out of the office.

"Oh, Glory," she said aloud to herself, "what have you gotten yourself into?"

* * *

Bram hummed along with a peppy country-western song playing on the radio in his Blazer.

He was definitely in a fine mood—better than fine. Yes, sir, he was flying high, and with just cause. He was on his way to pick up the lovely lady he would spend the evening with, due to an expertly executed, genius-level scheme.

Of course, he still had to convince Glory to agree to the whole proposal. One hamburger did not a victory make. But so far he was doing great, and his confidence was at the maximum.

"You're awesome, Bishop," he said aloud, as he maneuvered through the heavy traffic.

In the next instant, he frowned.

It was obvious that Glory was a stickler for details, as evidenced by her "your place, or mine?" query. He'd bet a buck that one of her first questions would be just how long they were to play out their pretend marriage.

What should he go for? A month? No, he'd better play it safe. Two weeks. He might have trouble selling Glory on a month, but two weeks would be a piece of cake.

"Awesomely awesome," Bram said, then began to whistle along with the song on the radio.

Glory wandered around her small living room, her eyes narrowed in deep concentration.

She'd had most of the afternoon to think about Bram's proposed plan, since she hadn't been fully booked with clients. And the more she thought about smooth-talking Mr. Bishop, the more she smelled a rat.

There was a distinct possibility, she'd concluded finally, that she was smack-dab in the middle of a scam. She *still* found it hard to believe that a man with the looks, build and charm of Bram Bishop needed help in his approach to a serious relationship with a woman.

Then why the elaborate charade he was attempting to put into motion? Because she hadn't fallen all over him, pressed a piece of paper into his hand on the airplane, batted her eyelashes and gushed "Call me, big boy."

It could very well be that Bram viewed her as a challenge, a break in the boredom of his having any woman he wanted. His prenuptial training idea was a bunch of malarkey. Yes, the longer she thought about it, the more sense that conclusion made.

So why was she waiting for Bram's arrival so they could further discuss his plan? Because the whole idea had merit and could be highly beneficial in building her client list.

Bram would never know she was wise to his duplicity. He'd enjoy his fun and games, she'd gain valuable data for future prenuptial counseling, and a good time would be had by all. Excellent.

As for her unsettling reaction to Bram, she was home free. She was aware of the effect he'd *had*—past tense—on her and, therefore, would now be immune to his masculine magnetism. Fine.

So, how long a period of time should she agree to partake in this scheme? A month? Oh, heaven forbid. She'd be a basket case if her life was topsy-turvy for that many days. She liked order and consistency in her existence.

Two weeks. She'd negotiate carefully, and they'd settle on two weeks, with Bram never knowing what hit him.

Goodness, she was sharp. She was squaring off against a high roller of the singles scene and was holding her own and then some.

She was one step ahead of slick Mr. Bram Bishop.

Bram drove slowly down the quiet street, glancing left and right as he looked at the houses. It was an old, established neighborhood made up of small homes that were obviously tended with loving care.

As he pulled into Glory's driveway, Bram mentally agreed with her depiction of her house as a cottage.

It was painted country blue with white shutters and had a wooden swing suspended by chains on the front porch. Daffodils edged the sidewalk leading to the steps; the grass was green and appeared freshly mowed, and a mulberry tree shaded the house from one side of the yard.

Cute place, Bram thought, nodding in approval. And *cute* was a good word to describe it. He also liked what it represented. Glory Carson had searched for a house, not an apartment, when she'd arrived in Houston. That had domestic connotations. Very good.

Bram got out of his vehicle and walked carefully on the round stepping-stones leading across the grass to the sidewalk. Once on the porch he pressed the bell, anticipating the moment when Glory Carson would appear at the door.

* * *

Glory jumped at the sound of the doorbell buzzing. She'd been so engrossed in her thoughts that she hadn't heard a car approaching her house. She took a steadying breath and crossed the room while producing, she hoped, a pleasant smile.

She was admittedly a tad nervous about the evening ahead. She would soon be engaging in a charade of her own by seemingly agreeing to Bram's plan as he was presenting it. That she was wise to *his* charade was something he mustn't be cognizant of.

She'd never done anything remotely deceptive before, but for the sake of her career, she'd pull it off. Somehow.

Glory opened the door, then unlatched the outer screen.

"Hello, Bram," she said, totally forgetting to smile. "Come in."

Oh, drat, she thought. Bram looked even better than he had in her office earlier that day. The crisp, new jeans had been replaced by soft, faded ones that hugged his hips and legs to the point of sinfulness. The white Western shirt was now a blue one that matched his eyes to perfection. That was not fair!

Bram stepped into the living room, a slight frown on his face.

"Good evening, Glory," he said, his gaze flickering over her. "You're running late? Hey, no problem. I'll wait while you change."

Glory cocked her head to one side in confusion. "Pardon me?"

"Your clothes." Bram swept one hand toward her.

"You're wearing what you had on at your office. This is a casual outing, remember?"

Glory glanced down at her attire, then met Bram's gaze again.

"Oh," she said. "Well, casual clothing is what a person is comfortable in. I'm really quite comfortable dressed as I am."

So much for seeing Glory in jeans, Bram thought. Scratch the hope that she might have her hair falling free. Man, what was it going to take to get Glory to loosen up? She was most comfortable in a business suit? Geez.

"Nice place," Bram said, deciding not to comment further on Glory's clothes. He glanced around the room. "Did you move your furniture here from Chicago, or did you rent, buy, this place furnished?"

"I'm renting and this is my furniture," she said. "Coming here was a big change in my life, and I wanted familiar things around me." She laughed. "I'm attempting to view this room fresh, through your eyes. I guess it's apparent that I like flowers."

Bram nodded, unable to curb a smile at the sound of Glory's lilting laughter.

The furniture in the small living room was a splash of bright, cheerful colors. Two easy chairs and a love seat had been upholstered in multicolored wildflowers against a white background. The coffee and end tables were gleaming oak.

"I imagine," Bram said, "that the flowers perked you up during the long, dreary Chicago winters."

"Yes," she said, "they really did. I'm surprised— Well, I'm surprised you thought of that. You know, seeing my choices as more than frilly, feminine furniture.''

"It's that, too," he said, smiling at her. "But I decorated my place in color tones that represent Texas to me. It's not to everyone's taste, I'm sure, but the aura of Texas brings me a sense of peace and contentment."

"I'm still Chicago Glory, I guess, pepping myself up with spring flowers in here, when I actually have some growing in my front yard. You're definitely Texas Bram, born here, loving it here.''

"Don't you like living in Texas?" Bram asked, his smile vanishing.

"I'm adjusting.. slowly. It's a tremendous change from Chicago. The weather, the easygoing attitudes of the people, the belief that tomorrow is soon enough, and the list goes on. It's very different from the frantic pace I'm accustomed to."

"But you're going to stay," Bram said, in the form of a firm statement, not a question.

"Definitely. I'm determined to adapt. Plus, starting a professional practice from scratch in a new location is no small chore. I certainly don't want to do it again.''

"Well, good. That's settled then. Ready to go?"

The first vibrant streaks of a sunset were just beginning to materialize as Glory and Bram left the house and walked to his vehicle. Bram opened the door and assisted Glory up onto the rather high seat of the Blazer.

"Hmm," Bram said, not closing the door. "This

isn't exactly the enchanting chariot I'd need if I were going to take my wife out for a special evening of dining and dancing. What do you think?''

"Me?'' Glory said. "Oh, well, it would be great for a family outing, such as a picnic, and it's very roomy for grocery shopping day. One would assume that your...your wife would have a car. You could use her vehicle for the fancier events.''

Bram looked at Glory's compact car that was parked in the driveway in front of the Blazer. He nodded and smiled at Glory.

"Makes sense to me,'' he said, then closed the door.

This, Glory thought, was going to take some getting used to.

They were soon caught up in the surging traffic, Glory aware that Bram drove with relaxed expertise.

"So, did you give some more thought to my plan?'' Bram said.

"Yes, I did. I think it has a lot of potential and...and I'm willing to give it a try.''

Bingo! Bram thought.

"However, Bram,'' Glory said, "I must insist on a predetermined length of time we're going to engage in this program.'' Two weeks, and not one day longer, she reminded herself.

Uh-oh, Bram thought. Were they about to go to battle? He was going to dig in his heels and hold out for two weeks, not a day less.

"Okay,'' Bram said. "We'll negotiate. My first offer is a month.''

"My counteroffer,'' Glory said, "is one week.''

"Two and a half weeks.''

"Two weeks," Glory said.

"Sold. Two weeks, it is," Bram said. You're sharp, Bishop, very sharp.

Nice work, Dr. Carson, Glory thought smugly.

"That was easy enough," Bram said. "We discussed the matter like adults, expressed ourselves clearly and compromised." Wrong. He hadn't compromised. He'd gotten exactly what he wanted.

Whatever, Glory thought. The truth of the matter was she'd outmaneuvered him, and they'd sealed their bargain with the time frame *she'd* chosen.

Bram glanced over at Glory and they exchanged I'm-very-pleased-with-myself smiles.

"By the way," Bram said, redirecting his attention to the traffic, "you know that list you spoke of that has the most frequent causes of divorce?"

"Yes."

"What's the biggy? Number one? The thing that blows most people apart?"

"A breakdown," Glory said, "in communication."

Four

Bram chose a family restaurant, and once they were seated inside, he urged Glory to have a steak if she wished, saying "going out for a hamburger" had been a figure of speech. Glory settled on fried shrimp in a basket, while Bram ordered the biggest steak offered on the menu.

When their dinners were set in front of them, they ate in silence for several minutes.

"Delicious," Bram said finally. "How's your shrimp and fries?"

"Very good," Glory said. "I'll ditto your *delicious.*"

"I realize the purpose of this evening is to discuss the possibility of embarking on my plan. Since we've already agreed to do it..." Bram shrugged.

"Well, there are a few details to cover," Glory said.

"Like when do we start, how will we divide the two weeks between your place and mine, the matter of expenses."

Bram smiled. "You sure do have a mind for details. I could use you as a foreman on one of my construction crews." He paused. "Why don't we begin tomorrow?"

"Start with a weekend?" Glory frowned. "I don't think that's a good idea, Bram. That would throw us together for two full days right off the bat. I believe we should ease into this a bit. Why don't we meet after work on Monday at my house?"

"Well…yes, okay. You have a cautious nature, don't you? You don't jump into things without taking a long, hard look."

"I try not to. I'm not a risk taker, I guess."

Bram looked at Glory intently. "Marriage is a risk. There are no etched-in-stone guarantees, no matter how much you want it to be forever love, no matter how hard you concentrate on it."

"You'll notice I'm not married." Glory took another bite of shrimp.

Alarm bells went off in Bram's head.

"Wait a minute," he said, sinking back in his chair. "Are you saying you're a marriage counselor who doesn't intend to get married?"

Glory stared into space for a long moment.

"That about covers it," she said, nodding.

"Ah-ha," Bram said, "I get the picture. You've dealt so long with people whose marriages are a terrible mess that you're a victim of your daily professional environment. Your career has made you prejudiced against the institution of marriage.''

''Wrong. I decided long ago to remain single, *then* selected my specialty. It's my deepest desire to help people be happy together and to create a serene, loving home for them and for any children they might have, or plan to have in the future.''

''Nice spiel. But why don't you want the same thing for yourself? Glory, before you answer that, think about the list, the importance of communication. Talk to me, share with me here.''

Glory frowned. ''We're not starting our togetherness number until Monday evening.''

Bram leaned forward. ''Don't nitpick. This is important. I'm your husband, remember? I'm supposed to know all about you. That includes your hopes, dreams, secrets...good or bad...the whole nine yards.''

''I never agreed to bare my soul to you,'' she said, her voice rising.

''How can I learn to be a proper husband if I don't know everything about my wife? The things that make her smile, the things that make her sad? I need practice in dealing with emotions other than my own.''

''Lower your voice,'' Glory whispered. ''People are beginning to stare at us.''

''So what?''

''Bram, the second item on the list of causes of divorce is infidelity. That doesn't need discussion. A person stays true to their marriage vows, pure and simple. But the third reason for breakups? Constant fighting. We're squabbling already.''

"Excellent point. This squabble, as you call it, will cease to exist as soon as you tell me why you have a mind-set against marriage."

Glory sighed. "That's it. Let's cancel the whole arrangement."

"Not a chance. We have a deal."

Glory pushed her dinner to one side, her appetite having vanished.

"All right...I guess. My reasoning is nothing fancy, Bram. I'm an only child born to parents who were contemplating divorce when a surprise—me—popped onto the scene. I grew up in a house filled with tension, loud arguments between my parents, hateful, screaming accusations, doors slamming, dishes breaking."

"I'm sorry, Glory," Bram said quietly.

"I can recall burying my head under my pillow when I was a little girl, trying not to hear them," she said, staring at her place mat. "I spent more than one night in the closet, covering my ears with my hands, just crying and crying."

Bram reached over to clasp one of Glory's hands on top of the table. "That's so rotten. I truly am sorry you went through that, Glory."

Glory reluctantly lifted her gaze to meet Bram's, her breath catching as she looked directly into his blue eyes.

"You...you really are sorry," she said, an incredulous tone to her voice. "I can see it in your eyes, on your face."

"Why are you surprised?"

"I don't know. I've never told anyone about my

childhood before. I never considered what someone's reaction might be.''

"If I'm your husband, I'm also supposed to be your best friend. I care, Glory, but not because I'm playing some role at the moment for our plan. I care as a person, a man, who hates the vision in my mind of that lonely, frightened little girl. I wish it had all been different for you. I wish you had terrific parents like I have.''

"Thank you, Bram," she said softly.

Seconds ticked by. They didn't move. A large, tanned, work-roughened hand covered a soft, small hand on top of a wooden table in a noisy restaurant. Eyes of emerald green and sapphire blue transmitted and received gentle messages of understanding, compassion, a bit of trust, a great deal of warmth.

It was all so very, very special.

"More coffee?" a waitress said, appearing suddenly at their table.

"Oh," Glory gasped, jerking in her chair. She snatched her hand from beneath Bram's.

"I didn't mean to startle you, honey," the waitress said. "Coffee?"

"No, thank you," Glory said.

Bram shook his head and the woman hurried to the next table.

"Anyway," Glory said, now looking at her coffee cup, "I made up my mind when I was in high school that I would major in psychology in college, become a marriage counselor and hopefully make it possible for children not to grow up in an environment like mine. End of story.''

"And your parents?"

"Oh, they're still together, still hollering at each other."

"But you know what it takes to make a marriage work, Glory. A child of yours would never have cause to cry in the closet."

"Oh? How do I know that, Bram? Look at the two of us." She swept one hand in the air. "We started bickering. That certainly wasn't our intention when we came in here, but it happened."

She shook her head.

"My parents didn't say to each other, 'Hey, let's get married and engage in a lifetime of quarrels, the louder the better,' but that's how it has been. I'm not running that risk. If I'm alone, I can control the atmosphere within my home."

"But…"

Glory produced a small smile. "All is not lost. I'll be a wife for the next two weeks. I won't ever have to feel I missed out on the experience."

"Cute," Bram said, frowning.

"I've made my choices, Bram. I'm very fulfilled by helping people straighten out their problems. I make a difference…to them, to their children. I'm very grateful for that."

"Glory, look—"

"Bram," she said, patting his hand where it was still splayed on top of the table, "the subject is closed. We're both going to have to use our imaginations during the next weeks to envision me as your wife, because in actuality I never intend to be one." She paused. "I wonder what they offer for dessert here?"

* * *

Late that night Bram lay in bed unable to sleep. He felt as though there was a tape recorder in his head, replaying over and over what Glory had told him about her childhood and her stand of never marrying.

Each time he saw, in his mind's eye, that frightened little girl crying in the closet because her parents were arguing yet again, a cold fist tightened in his gut.

He hated the fact that Glory had grown up under such dreadful circumstances. She'd lived in a house, not a home filled with laughter and love. That was sad.

But his sympathy changed quickly to frustration when he remembered her wish never to marry.

How could a supposedly intelligent woman, one who *specialized* in marriage counseling, have such rigid and unrealistic opinions?

Marriage was too risky? There were no guarantees it would be sweet bliss? It didn't come with a money-back warranty, so she'd pass, thank you very much? Cripe, what an attitude.

"Man, oh, man," Bram said, dragging his hands down his face, "now what do I do?"

He dropped his arms heavily onto the bed and narrowed his eyes.

As of Monday evening, Glory Carson would be his wife, and he would be her husband. He had two weeks to observe her in that role and decide if she was a viable wife candidate. He'd have to see through any wifely performing she might be doing for the sake of research. He'd watch carefully and decide if her actions flowed naturally, or if they were what she felt she *should* be doing.

He also had only two weeks to convince Glory that having a husband hanging around the house wasn't a rotten way to live. Because if he concluded that he wanted Glory as his *real* wife, it sure would help his cause if he'd changed—however slightly—her 'I never intend to marry' mind-set.

Bram yawned. The thing was the two weeks had to have an aura of authenticity to them. Bringing home flowers and candy every night wasn't realistic.

The best way to handle this was to just be himself, do what felt natural and right. He'd given Blue that advice about Amy at one point, and now his brother, the lucky devil, was married to the woman of his heart, his forever love.

Yep, Bram concluded, as sleep edged over his senses, he'd just be Bram Bishop, the man, come Monday evening.

No, he'd be Bram Bishop, the *husband*.

Glory rinsed out the mug that had held warm milk, set it in the sink, then shuffled down the hall to her bed. Back beneath her covers, she sighed, hoping she'd now be able to sleep.

She kept hearing herself telling Bram about her childhood, and cringed as the words echoed over and over in her head.

Why had she done that? She'd *never* divulged the secrets of her youth to anyone, not during high school, college or beyond. Why had she blurted it all out to Bram? And even worse, why had she felt so warm, so comforted, when he'd looked at her with those beautiful blue eyes and said, "I'm sorry, Glory"?

Okay, what was done couldn't be erased. Going over it a zillion times wasn't going to allow her to get the sleep she needed. So Bram knew about her childhood. Big deal.

She really wished, though, that she hadn't made herself eligible for the Miss Chatter Cheeks of the Year award. Telling Bram she never intended to marry had no doubt heightened the level of challenge she represented.

Bram wouldn't want to demolish her stand on the issue so *he* could marry her, but his giant-size male ego wouldn't approve of her saying that no man could change her mind.

Now Bram had two goals. To make her fall prey to his masculine magnetism because thus far—shame on her—she hadn't. *And* to reverse her attitude and make her believe that being married to a member of the male species would be the greatest thing since sliced bread.

"Ohhh, Glory," she said aloud, "sometimes you talk too much, you really do."

All that aside, the question remained of how she would behave beginning on Monday evening when she became Bram's wife. How was she to act, perform, once they were past "Honey, I'm home"?

Drat it, she didn't know. She'd never been a wife before. Oh, forget it. She would just be herself and observe Bram's reactions. That was the kind of information she needed to be gathering for future prenuptial counseling of clients.

That Bram's behavior would probably be as phony

as a three-dollar bill in his attempt to accomplish his goals was unimportant.

So be it. She had it all figured out.

Glory closed her eyes and slept.

Sunday evening, Bram, Blue and Tux sat on the deck at the back of Tux and Nancy's home.

Blue raised his can of beer in the air. "To the Bishop boys."

"Hear, hear," Tux said, lifting his can.

Bram clinked his can against the other two. "And to their wives."

All three men took a deep swallow of beer to acknowledge the toast.

"Well," Tux said, "it certainly will be interesting to hear how this plan of yours goes, Bram. Maybe there will be three Bishop wives to toast one of these days."

"It sure is complicated, though, Bram," Blue said. "What happens if Glory discovers you were conning her? You know, were zeroing in on her from the get-go, not really in husband boot camp, as you put it."

"How would she ever find out?" Bram asked.

"Beginning a relationship based on a lie isn't great," Tux said.

"Hey, what choice do I have? Glory is so dead set against getting married, that I doubt she'd agree to go out on more than two or three dates with me. She wouldn't run the risk of having any serious feelings for me sneak up on her.

"But for the next two weeks, she *has* to spend every

evening with me. I swear, I amaze myself sometimes with my brilliant ideas.''

"Oh, right," Tux said dryly. "What happened to the appropriate-behavior number? Living a lie is *not* appropriate behavior."

"Would you quit harping on the lie thing?" Bram said, glaring at Tux. "Think of it as a *plan* to get to know a beautiful, intelligent woman better than I know her now. So far, she's a perfect ten."

"Yeah, well, I pulled a scam on Amy, remember?" Blue said. "I got her boss at the newspaper, Gibson McKinley, to send Amy on assignments that would make her see the wonderfulness of hearth, home and babies. When Amy found out what I did—hell, I was dead meat, totally toast.''

"But Amy came around," Bram said. "She realized what you had done was based on love. Besides, Glory will never find out that I didn't need husband training, and was only doing a deal to be near her."

"Ho-ho, listen to this," Tux said. "You've got the husband bit down pat? I've got news for you, little brother. It's not that simple. Why? Because in order to be a husband, you have to have a wife. A wife is a woman. And they are very complicated creatures, those women people.''

"Amen," Blue said.

"Oh." Bram frowned. "Well, okay, you guys, give me some tips. As of tomorrow evening, I'm a husband.''

"Should we help out here, Tux?" Blue said.

"No."

"Thanks a helluva lot, Tux," Bram said.

"I still think you're making a big mistake by lying to Glory." Tux shook his head. "You should listen to me, because I'm older and, therefore, wiser than you."

"Not," Bram said, chuckling. "One year older doesn't count for squat."

"Don't say I didn't warn you about your lack of truth, Bishop," Tux said.

"I hear you, Bishop. Now come on, what's the inside scoop on being a husband?"

"Yeah, okay," Blue said. "Be wary of any conversation that starts with, 'I need to talk to you.'"

"Don't tell her she looks fine if she says she feels fat," Tux said.

"Do not *ever*," Blue said, "let the words 'What's for dinner?' be the first thing out of your mouth when you arrive home."

"If she asks you 'What's wrong?,' come up with something, *anything*," Tux said, "but don't shrug and say, 'Nothing.' That's like waving a red flag in front of a bull."

"Whew," Bram said. "This is beginning to sound a bit more intricate than I thought."

"Oh, they're something, these women, these wives," Blue said, "but I sure would hate to be going through life without my Amy."

"Or without my Incredibly Beautiful Nancy," Tux said, then glanced at his watch. "They should be back from the concert anytime now."

"Maybe I should ask Amy and Nancy for tips on being a husband," Bram said.

"Naw," Blue said. "What could they tell you? *We're* not the ones who are complicated. Once they get us shaped up a bit, living with us is a breeze, compared to our learning how to live with *them*."

"Amen," Tux said.

After a Monday that had seemed like three Mondays rolled into one, Glory drove toward home, the rush hour traffic appearing especially heavy.

It had taken all of her concentration to devote her full professional attention and abilities to her clients during the long, long day. She'd continually had to pull her mind back from the realization that after work she would acquire a husband in the form of Mr. Bram Bishop.

"Absurd," she muttered.

No, it wasn't, not really. The insights she would gain from the endeavor she was about to embark upon would be invaluable in the professional arena. She *knew* that, but still her mind was muddled.

Glory, stop it, she admonished herself. She'd spent the weekend going back and forth on the subject like a Ping-Pong ball. Enough was enough. The decision had been made.

"Let the games begin," she said, then laughed.

Was she getting hysterical? Totally losing it? That was very possible. Would Bram already be at her house when she arrived? If so, what would he be doing? As the husband, would he be slouched on the sofa waiting for his dinner to be prepared?

Glory's eyes widened, then she laughed again.

If her *husband* had reached the house before her, he would be sitting in his vehicle in the driveway or perched on the swing on the front porch. She and

Bram had not given one thought to exchanging keys to their respective abodes.

Glory frowned.

She had never in her life given the key to her home, her safe haven, to a man. And here she was, about to do just that with a man she barely knew. Dear heaven, this really *was* absurd.

"Oh, stop, stop, stop," she said aloud. "You're becoming very tiresome, Glory Carson."

Glory turned onto her street, her heart quickening as she slowed the speed of the car. She leaned forward, attempting to see if Bram's vehicle was at her house. Moments later she pulled into the empty driveway and drew a steadying breath.

Bram hadn't arrived yet, she thought, exiting her car. She had a slight reprieve, a few more minutes to collect her scattered nerves and get into a wife mode.

Wife mode? her mind echoed, as she unlocked the front door. She certainly could use a manual or instruction sheet of some kind.

After retrieving the mail from the box mounted on the porch wall next to the door, she entered the house.

In the past two days she'd tossed around a zillion times the fact that she'd never been a wife and had no clue as to what a wife would do. The conclusion she'd come to...continually...was that she would simply be herself, behave as she normally would.

"Okay," she said decisively. "Fine."

She took off her shoes, dropped them onto the floor, set her purse on a chair, then sank onto the sofa to examine the mail.

"Oh, Lord," she said an instant later.

She'd just heard a vehicle pull into her driveway. A door was slamming. Now—yes, there they were—footsteps on the porch. The screen was creaking, the doorknob was turning, the front door was opening and...Bram entered!

Staying put, her back to Bram, Glory stared at an envelope as though it was the most fascinating thing she'd ever seen.

"Hi, Glory," Bram said, "I'm here. I mean, I'm home."

"Hi," she said, still concentrating on the envelope.

"I realized on the way over here," Bram said, "that we should have given each other our spare house keys so that— What? Oh, man!"

Glory spun around to see a filthy Bram staring down at the floor.

"What's wrong?" she said.

"I just smashed a shoe to smithereens."

"What!" Glory jumped to her feet, causing the mail to fly in all directions. She rushed to where Bram was standing. "My new shoes. What am I supposed to do with only one? How could you do such a thing?"

Bram scowled. "Hey, it wasn't difficult. It's pretty easy to step on something that's left on the floor where it doesn't belong."

Glory planted her hands on her hips. "Most people watch where they're walking."

"Most people keep their shoes in the closet."

They stood there, matching glare for glare, as seconds ticked by.

"Hell," Bram said finally. "What a lousy start."

"No joke."

"Okay, let's regroup. I now know that my...wife takes off her shoes the instant she enters the house after work. It's up to me not to step on them and kill them."

"Indeed," Glory said, folding her arms beneath her breasts.

"Back up a minute. I just came in the door, and you've come to greet me."

"I have?"

"Well, yeah. Geez, Glory, it wouldn't be very wifely to have your nose buried in the mail and hardly acknowledge my arrival after a hard day on the job."

"Oh. Yes, of course, you're right." Her gaze skittered over him. "You're very grungy."

"I know. I brought clean clothes, but I forgot to bring them in. I'll shower and change."

"You're going to take a shower?" she said, a funny little squeak in her voice. "Here?"

"I live here, remember?"

Glory pressed one hand to her forehead. "I can't handle this."

"Yes, you can. It's just a matter of adjusting." Bram paused. "Where were we? Oh, yeah, I came in the door and you're welcoming me home." He paused again. "Well?"

"Well what?"

"Welcome me, for crying out loud."

"Oh. Okay. Welcome home, Bram."

"Thanks, sweetheart," he said, "it's good to be here."

Then Bram slipped one hand to the nape of Glory's neck, lowered his head and kissed her.

Five

Glory was so stunned by the sudden feel of Bram's lips on hers that she just stood there, pencil stiff, arms at her sides, eyes as wide as saucers.

But as Bram deepened the kiss by slipping his tongue between her lips, her lashes drifted down, and she met his questing tongue with her own.

Bram dropped his hand from Glory's neck to wrap both arms around her, nestling her to his rugged body. Glory's hands floated upward to encircle his neck, her fingertips inching into his thick hair.

Oh, my, Glory thought dreamily, it had been so long since she'd been held, been kissed. So very long. Even more, this kiss was exquisite, like none before, consuming her instantly with such heated desire it was as though her bones were melting from the licking flames.

She felt so alive, so womanly. Bram was the epitome of man, and she was femininity personified. It was ecstasy, this kiss. She wanted it to go on, and on and—

Bram jerked his head up and released his hold on Glory so quickly that she swayed on her feet.

"There," he said, his voice gritty. "I'm officially home and welcomed. I'll go get my clean clothes out of the Blazer."

He spun around, opened the door and strode out of the house. On the porch, he gave mental directives to his booted feet.

"Left foot," he muttered. "Right foot. Move, Bishop. You can do it."

When he reached the vehicle, he opened the driver's door, then turned and sank onto the seat, his feet on the gravel driveway.

He drew a deep breath, let it out very slowly, then splayed one hand on his still-racing heart.

Oh, man, he thought, shaking his head slightly. That kiss, that incredibly unbelievable kiss he'd just shared with Glory Carson, had caused an explosion of heated passion to rocket throughout him like nothing he'd ever experienced before.

Miss Prim-and-Proper-Always-the-Professional Dr. Carson was, without a doubt, the most sensuous, desirable woman he'd ever met.

The kiss was supposed to have been a little peck, a husbandly hello at the end of a workday. But at the very instant his lips had claimed the sweet honey of Glory's, he'd been lost, gone, swept away by a rushing current of wanting more, wanting Glory.

And now here he sat, weak in the knees, probably having a heart attack, and willing his aroused, aching body back under his command.

"Bishop, you idiot," he said, dragging both hands down his face. "You just blew it, big-time."

He'd bet a buck that the front door of Glory's house was now locked against his reentry, and that the whole deal was canceled.

Well, there was only one way to find out.

He reached behind the seat, grabbed his gym bag, then got out of the Blazer, slamming the door with more force than was necessary.

On the porch he hesitated, called himself six kinds of a coward, then swung back the screen door and turned the knob on the inner door.

The door opened.

Bram stepped tentatively into the living room, then stopped dead in his tracks, dropping his bag to the floor with a thud.

Glory was standing exactly where he'd left her, a rather bemused expression on her face. The entire front of her outfit was covered in dirt and cement dust from his work-dirty clothes.

Bram moved to stand directly in front of her.

"Bram," Glory said, looking at the center of his chest, "before you greet your wife upon your arrival home, I'd suggest you consider the condition of your clothing. You won't start out the evening on a serene footing if you've made it necessary for her to take her apparel to the cleaners."

"Right," he said, eyeing her warily.

"The shower is off my bedroom. Just go down the hall there."

Bram planted his hands on his hips. "That's it?" he said, none too quietly.

"Oh. There are clean towels in the linen cupboard in the hall."

"Damn it, Glory Carson, what about the kiss we just shared?"

Glory raised her eyebrows. "What about it?"

Bram inwardly fumed. He felt like a little kid, having brought home a picture he'd drawn at school and waiting for the hoorays from his mother.

What was Glory saying by saying nothing about that kiss? That it had been no big deal, an okay kiss, as far as kisses went, and wasn't worth commenting on?

Hadn't she been as sexually aroused as he had been? Hadn't she felt it? The heat? The explosion of desire beyond measure? Was he the only person in this room coming apart at the seams?

Bram glowered at Glory, really despising the pleasant, serene expression now on her face, then grabbed his bag and stomped down the hall.

Glory counted slowly to three after Bram disappeared from view, then wobbled over to the sofa and sank onto it heavily, crushing two envelopes from the day's mail.

Heavenly saints, she was dying. The heat still raging within her was going to totally dissolve her. She'd disappear off the face of the earth, never to be seen again.

She pressed her hands to her cheeks.

Steady, Glory, she told herself. Calm down. She'd

handled the situation just fine—very clinically, very professionally. Bram had no clue that his kiss had thrown her into a sensual tizzy. As far as he knew, he'd made no progress whatsoever in his goal to ultimately get her to succumb to his masculine sensuousness.

She was officially accepting what he'd done as a husband greeting his wife after work. If she pitched a fit about it, she would remove the authenticity from the research and diminish the specialness of married people in love coming together at day's end.

And if she threw a tantrum, Bram would realize that the kiss had had a tremendously potent effect on her, a fact she had no intention of revealing.

Bram had assured her that their pretend marriage would not include sex. She'd be a real stick-in-the-mud if she refused to allow even a simple kiss.

Simple? her mind echoed. Simple! Not even close. It had been ecstasy in its purest form. To Bram, Mr. Studmuffin, the kiss was probably just one more in a series numbering into the thousands.

But to her?

Glory jumped to her feet and tried in vain to brush away the dirt and dust from her clothes.

She wasn't going to think about that kiss anymore. What was done, was done. The kiss was now a thing of the past, a fleeting memory.

So far, she thought as she began to collect the scattered mail, she and Bram had managed to come home from work and greet each other. At this rate, she would never survive two whole weeks of this arrangement.

She had to get a grip on herself, remember that for now she was a psychologist first, a woman a distant second. The research she would be conducting over the following days would be very valuable.

But she now knew that she'd have to be very careful. While she was collecting information, she had no intention of losing her heart in the process.

Bram frowned as he snapped the clean Western shirt.

Tux and Blue, he mused, had sure been right on the money when they'd said that women—wives—were very complicated creatures.

The really strange thing was that while he'd been dating a slew of different women, not one of them had been the least bit complicated at all. Weird.

As far as he could tell, he could arrive home from work every evening for the next two weeks in his role of husband, sweep Glory into his arms and kiss her like there was no tomorrow.

That was fine with him—more than fine—but did it make sense that Glory wasn't stamping her foot and demanding he keep his hands and his kisses to himself? No, it certainly did not.

Glory had responded to that kiss, had kissed him as passionately as he'd been kissing her. But apparently it hadn't *meant* anything to her, seeing as that her only concern after their kiss had been the location of clean towels.

"Man," Bram said, stuffing his dirty clothes in the gym bag, "women are so strange, poor gorgeous things."

But be that as it may, he still wanted one to be his wife, his forever love. Soon. Very soon.

Bram left the bedroom, went into the now empty living room and set the bag by the door.

"Glory?" he called.

"Kitchen."

He crossed the small room to enter the minuscule kitchen beyond. Glory was standing in front of the refrigerator, staring into the freezer.

"Frozen dinners," she said. "Turkey? Meat Loaf? Pork?"

"Why don't we send out for a huge pizza?"

"It's not in our budget."

"It's not?" he said, frowning. "We don't have twenty bucks for a pizza?"

Glory closed the freezer and turned to look at Bram.

Oh, he was so handsome, she thought. His hair was damp from the shower, his rugged features bronzed to perfection by the sun.

She liked the varying shades of his hair, the sun-streaked places, then the warm brown. He was built just right for tapered Western shirts with his broad shoulders and chest, his flat stomach.

And what he did for a pair of jeans was enough to give a woman a case of the vapors.

"Hello?" Bram said. "Pizza?"

"Oh. No. No pizza. Bram, we're newly married, setting up housekeeping with all the expenses that entails. The seventh most common reason for divorce is money problems. It's not wise to fall into the habit of ordering in dinner, instead of cooking. Take-out food can be disastrous to a budget."

"Well, if you say so. Do we have any peanut butter and jelly?"

"Yes."

"Okay. I'll have one of those frozen dinners, then make myself three or four sandwiches."

Glory nodded, then took two dinners from the freezer and a head of lettuce from the crisper.

"Aren't you going to change your clothes?" Bram said.

"There's no point. I can't wear this suit to work again until it's cleaned, so I might as well leave it on."

"I'll pay for the cleaning bill, Glory." Bram inwardly sighed. Chalk up another day without seeing Glory in jeans, with her hair falling free. "I'm sorry I got that dust and dirt on you."

"That's all right. Would you set the table, please? Just open cupboards and drawers until you find what you need."

They busied themselves with their chores.

"You said money was the seventh reason for divorce," Bram said, putting silverware on the table. "You skipped a few on the list. We'd covered the first three—breakdown of communication, infidelity and constant arguing."

"Well," Glory said, placing a bowl of tossed salad on the table, "number four is emotional abuse, and number eight is physical abuse."

"Mmm," Bram said, nodding. "I remember one time when Tux, Blue and I were talking about guys who hit their wives, girlfriends, whatever. There's no excuse for it...none. Tux said if he ever saw a man hit a woman, he'd take the scum apart, even if he was a total stranger. But..."

Glory met Bram's troubled gaze.

"But?" she prompted.

"We all looked at each other after he'd said that. Blue and I had nodded in agreement right off. You know, figured we'd do exactly what Tux had said.

"But then we realized it was rather confusing. We'd show that son-of-a...gun he shouldn't hit a woman by beating the living daylights out of him? Was that the lesson we wanted to teach our future children?"

"Did you come up with an answer to that puzzle?"

"No. No, we really didn't."

"You and your brothers are very sensitive, very caring men, Bram."

"I don't know about that," he said, "but we came away from the conversation with one thing etched in stone, at least."

"Which is?"

"When a man is in love, knows that it's his forever love, he's very calmly, very completely prepared to lay his life on the line for his lady. No hesitation, no questions asked...just do it. He'd die for her in a New York minute, if necessary."

"I'll...I'll get some drinks," Glory said, hurrying across the room.

Dear heaven, she was struggling against threatening tears, she thought, as she took an ice cube tray from the freezer. She'd been touched deep within her being by Bram's declaration.

He hadn't spoken with any ring of machismo or verbal muscle flexing. It was simply a fact that the

Bishop boys would sacrifice their lives for their…their forever love, as they called it.

Bram Bishop knew how to love.

He'd been raised in a loving home, by loving parents, had been surrounded by loving brothers.

That did not, however, guarantee that he would make a good husband. That role took work on a daily basis and was made up of a multitude of little things.

Glory smiled as she dropped ice cubes into two glasses.

One of those things was not killing his wife's new shoes. Of course, said wife could certainly learn to be considerate enough not to leave her shoes in the middle of the floor.

Wait a minute, she thought. She was getting too caught up in this charade, had been reacting as though Bram was actually engaging in husband boot camp.

Oh, she didn't doubt that he wished to get married, but his challenge at the moment was to seduce her.

She *had* to remember that as she conducted her research.

She had some information already and would now be more sympathetic to clients with money problems, who complained that they only had so much energy, and take-out food was easier than cooking. She'd suggest that they prepare the meals together, sharing the load.

She'd also recommend a better balanced meal than frozen dinners and peanut butter and jelly sandwiches!

Glory and Bram ate the rather makeshift meal while chatting about books they'd read, the three buildings

Bram's company had in various stages of construction, and the fact that Houston could use some rain.

After cleaning the kitchen, they wandered into the living room.

"Well, here we are," Glory said, aware that she was suddenly a tad nervous. "An evening at home."

"At the 'Bishops'," Bram said, sitting down on one end of the sofa. "Did you change your name?"

Glory settled onto the other end of the sofa. "Pardon me?"

"When we got married, did you change your name to Bishop?"

"I... Well, I don't know. I guess I would use Bishop on a personal level. You know, on our joint checking account for paying the bills, buying the groceries. I'd keep Carson in my professional arena."

Bram nodded. "Sounds fair." He paused. "So, what would you normally do during an evening like this?"

"I might get caught up on paperwork from the office or read a psychology journal. Other nights I see if there's a movie I'd like to watch on television or enjoy a novel."

"Do you ever get lonely?"

Glory opened her mouth to reply in the negative, then closed it again, frowning slightly.

"I think," she finally said slowly, "that anyone who lives alone has moments when they wish there was someone to talk to, share with. That's only natural.

"But in the overall picture...no, I'm not lonely, because I chose my life-style. It wasn't forced on me by divorce or death. You might be more conscious of your aloneness because you've decided to marry and haven't yet found the right woman.''

"That makes sense," Bram said.

"How do you spend your evenings, Bram?"

"Oh, watch the tube, read a book, whatever."

"What would you like to do now?"

Dr. Carson, Bram thought, swallowing a chuckle, that was not a wise question to ask a healthy, red-blooded man who was still feeling the lingering effects of a very sensational kiss shared with a very desirable woman.

"Who does your yard work?" he asked.

"I hire a high school boy from down the street to tend to it."

"Can we afford that?"

"It's not a luxury like ordering in pizza. I simply don't have the time or energy to keep up the outside, as well as the inside, of the house."

Bram smiled. "I'll take care of the yard, and we'll use the money we save to buy a pizza."

"You're determined to have that pizza, aren't you, Bram Bishop?" Glory said, laughing. "Do you always get what you want?"

Bram looked directly at Glory, no trace of a smile left on his face.

"Usually," he said. "It depends on how badly I want it."

Oh, mercy, Glory thought, those eyes, those sapphire blue eyes of Bram's were spellbinding. When he looked at her as intensely as he was now, she was consumed by a rush of heated desire, of burning want and need like nothing she'd experienced before in her entire life.

Glory tore her gaze from Bram's and got to her feet.

"I...I think we should call it a night," she said. "We can pretend we agreed to watch television or sit quietly and read. We discussed it, one of us might have compromised, and we're settled in until it's time to go...to go to bed."

"Glory—"

"There's no reason to actually live out these hours, as long as we know there was no discord in determining—"

"Glory—"

"What!" she said, nearly shrieking.

"Do I make you nervous?" Bram asked quietly.

"Of course you make me nervous," she said, flinging out her arms. "I'm not exactly a veteran at spending quiet evenings at home with one of the sexiest men who ever put on a pair of pants and—"

Glory's eyes widened in horror.

"Oh, Lord," she said, "I did *not* say that."

She pressed her hands to her flushed cheeks.

Bram got to his feet, closed the distance between them, then gently gripped Glory's shoulders. She stared at a pearly snap on his shirt.

"Glory," he said, "look at me."

"No. I'm mortified. I can't believe how unprofessionally I—"

"Hey, forget professional for a minute, would you, please? Look at me."

Glory sighed and raised her eyes to meet Bram's gaze.

"This is all new to me, too, you know," he said. "Normally if I was with a beautiful, very desirable woman like you, there'd be more going on than reading a book or counting the flowers on the sofa."

"That's disgusting."

"No, that's a fact, pure and simple. We'd be making love, Glory Carson. Sweet, slow love. Kissing. Touching. Then—"

"Stop it, Bram," she whispered, a shiver coursing through her.

"You're right," he said, dropping his hands to his sides. "I'm driving myself up the wall." He exhaled a puff of air. "Okay. I'm fine now." He paused. "No, I'm not, but I'll ignore it.

"Glory, listen, what we're actually doing here is communicating extremely well. We now know that we're attracted to each other, find each other desirable and… Enough said about *that*."

"I wholeheartedly agree."

"Except for one thing."

"Which is?"

"We have the facts on the subject. The unanswered question that's floating through the air is—what are we going to do about that sexual pull?"

Before Glory could reply, Bram dropped a quick kiss on her lips.

"Good night, Glory. I'm positive I thoroughly enjoyed my quiet evening reading a book, with you next to me reading yours. I'll see you tomorrow evening…same time, same place. We'll go grocery shopping. How's that? Great. 'Bye."

Bram spun around, strode across the room, picked up his gym bag and left the house.

"But…" Glory said, raising one finger in the air.

"Whatever," she said in the next instant, throwing up her hands.

She sank onto the sofa, realized she was exhausted and closed her eyes.

Well, she'd survived the first evening of the prenuptial training...sort of. She couldn't even be certain if it had been all that productive, because the whole program was brand-new, with no measuring stick of progress to use.

What are we going to do about that sexual pull?

Glory's eyes flew open as Bram's words echoed in her mind.

"Nothing," she said aloud. "We're going to *do* absolutely nothing about it, Mr. Bishop."

With a derisive I'm-back-in-control-of-the-situation nod, Glory got to her feet, went to the bathroom and took a long, relaxing bubble bath.

In his apartment Bram flicked on the television, then slouched into his favorite chair.

Everything was going great so far, he thought, smiling rather smugly. He now knew that Glory was as attracted to him as he was to her.

He'd even maneuvered things around so that she was left with the question of where that sexual tension between them might lead. She couldn't help but think about what the answer might be.

To top it off, his coup de grace had been confirming plans to go grocery shopping so he wouldn't starve to death during the training program.

Man, oh, man, it sure felt good knowing he was in control of the situation.

Six

Bram stopped pushing the grocery cart and planted his hands on his hips.

"Come on, Glory," he said, "we have to have snacks in the house. How am I supposed to get through the evening without something to munch on? Everyone has a snack cupboard."

Glory narrowed her eyes and leaned slightly toward him.

"A snack *shelf*, maybe," she said, "but *not* an entire cupboard. We're on a tight budget, remember?"

"That does it," Bram said. "We have enough food for a couple of nights. This shopping trip is over, because you and I need to talk."

"But—"

"We're out of here, Glory," Bram said, spinning the cart around. "Unless, of course, you want to have a squabble right here among the pretzels and potato chips.'' He started down the aisle.

''Well!'' Glory said, with an indignant sniff.

Bram turned a corner and disappeared from view.

''Oh, dear,'' Glory said, then hurried after him.

At the check-out counter, Bram paid for the groceries, lifted the heavy sack into the crook of one arm, then headed for the door of the store.

Glory took one look at the tight set of Bram's jaw and decided to keep quiet until they were in her living room.

As Bram drove out of the mall's parking lot, Glory slid another glance at him from beneath her lashes.

Was Bram actually throwing a tantrum over a bag of pretzels? she thought incredulously. Oh, surely not. There had to be something else wrong, something brewing inside him, that had just happened to erupt in the snack aisle of the store. Right? Well, she had a feeling that when they got home, she was definitely going to find out.

When they got home, her mind echoed. There was no denying the fact that during the day at the office, she'd thought, more times than she cared to count, about the fact that Bram would be waiting for her that evening when she arrived at the house.

The disturbing realization was that that scenario caused a warmth to suffuse her.

Bram had been sitting on the porch swing when she'd pulled into the driveway. Before they even entered the house, they finally remembered to exchange keys.

She could vividly recall the funny flutter that had

whispered down her spine as she'd placed her house key in Bram's outstretched hand.

Once in the living room, he'd encircled her with his arms and kissed her deeply. She'd been awash with instant desire, with heated, churning want that still thrummed low in her body.

"I'm home," Bram had said, when he finally released her.

"Welcome," was all she'd managed to say.

Glory sighed.

But right after that, something had gone off track. Bram had said they'd go grocery shopping as soon as she changed her clothes. She'd said she would just go to the store as she was, and he'd been as grumpy as a bear ever since.

What on earth was the matter with him?

At the house Bram carried the grocery sack into the kitchen and unpacked the food. Without speaking or touching, they put the groceries away.

"There," Bram said. "We are now going to communicate, darling wife."

He strode into the living room, but remained standing. Glory sat down on one end of the sofa and looked up at him questioningly.

"What seems to be the problem?" she asked, folding her hands primly in her lap. "Surely you're not this angry over a bag of pretzels or a jar of peanuts."

"Yes, as a matter of fact, I am," Bram said, none too quietly. "Why? Because you're dictating the terms of this marriage, Glory, and I've had enough of it."

"What are you talking about?" she said, her voice rising in volume.

"*You* decided we were a newly married couple on a very tight budget. We're counting every penny to the point that we can't even order in a damn pizza.

"Well, I've got news for you, Dr. Carson...no, correct that...Mrs. Bishop. I've worked very hard for many years to get Bishop Construction where it is today. I've earned the right, through back-breaking labor, to enjoy the extras in life."

"Oh, well, I—"

"I am one of the Bishop boys," Bram roared on, "and we provide the very best we possibly can for our wives. Have you got that? Don't tell *me* I can't afford to buy you a pretzel. You're not running this show, Glory, from A to Z, start to finish.

"On what page in a textbook does it say that all newly married couples are dead broke? What gives you the right to call the shots about everything we do?"

"But—"

"And another thing," Bram said. "Your clothes. Don't you own a pair of jeans, for Pete's sake? What is it going to take to get you to change out of your psychologist outfit and relax?" He nodded once sharply. "There. I've had my say. I *communicated.*"

Glory got to her feet, her green eyes flashing like lasers.

"No, you hollered." She flipped one hand in the air. "You stood there and ranted and raved. You call that communicating? Ha! It was a temper tantrum, a screamer, a pitch-a-fit."

"So what? I made my points clear, didn't I? You're

still doing it, Glory. Now you're deciding the acceptable method that I'm allowed to express my feelings."

"There's no need to yell," she yelled. "Ever!"

"Why not? Because your parents did it all the time when you were a kid? Did it ever occur to you to view them through fresh eyes now that you're an adult?

"You said your folks are still married. Why? Hey, maybe they actually love each other. Maybe they're just very volatile, demonstrative people. Okay, so it was upsetting to the child crying in the closet, but maybe, just maybe, you're standing in harsh judgment of their kind of forever love.

"Marriage isn't a chapter in a manual, Glory. It's real. Good times, bad, whispers of endearments when making love, and hollering your head off when you're pushed to the wall."

Bram thumped himself on the chest.

"Well, I'm at the wall, lady, with your counting pennies and telling me how I'm supposed to provide for my wife. *There will be pizza in this house, woman.*"

Glory opened her mouth, closed it, then sank onto the edge of the sofa, staring at Bram with wide eyes.

"I've...I've been a shrew? A nag?" she said, her voice trembling. "I'm a terrible wife? A dictator?"

"Oh, man," Bram said, dragging one hand through his hair. "You're making me feel so rotten for— No, you're not a terrible wife. You're just a bit... enthusiastic. There's nothing wrong here that we can't fix."

"But...but what if I'm *dictating* to my clients, instead of just making suggestions, giving advice? How many people are doing without pizza because I said they couldn't have any?''

Bram laughed and shook his head. "Trust me. They're sneaking a pizza into their kitchens in the dead of night.'' He went to the sofa and extended one hand to Glory. "Come here. Please?''

Glory tentatively placed one hand in Bram's and allowed him to ease her up and into his embrace.

"The thing about hollering is," he said, looking directly into her eyes, "it's hard to stop once you get started. Forget what I said about your parents. That was way out of line. You were there, lived through it.

"And, Glory? Don't start questioning your abilities as a marriage counselor. You're good, you know you are. It's just harder to be objective when you're the one who's in the marriage. We'll compromise. Okay? We'll be all right here."

"Okay," she said softly. "I'm sorry I said we had to pinch pennies. We should have discussed it."

"Well, I'm sorry I got carried away when I blew my stack."

Glory smiled. "Want to order in a giant pizza for dinner?"

"You bet." Bram began to lower his head toward hers. "In a minute."

Bram's mouth claimed Glory's, his tongue delving between her lips to meet and duel with her tongue.

Oh, yes, Bram's mind hummed. He *needed* this kiss and *wanted* this woman.

Yes, yes, Glory's mind whispered. The chill from arguing with Bram was gone, replaced by heat—burning, churning, pulsing. She couldn't think; she could only feel. She wanted Bram Bishop.

Bram lifted his head to draw a rough breath, then slanted his mouth in the other direction as he captured Glory's lips once again. He drank of her sweetness, inhaled her flowery aroma, relished the sensation of her breasts being crushed against the hard wall of his chest.

He could feel Glory surrendering to him, returning the kiss in total abandon, giving as much as she was receiving. Ah, Glory.

Bram's hands slid down over the gentle slope of Glory's bottom, cupping her womanly curves, nestling her to the cradle of his hips, his arousal heavy, aching.

He was slipping to the edge, losing control, the command over his body and mind. Slipping, slipping…closer and closer to oblivion—

Bram jerked his head up.

"No," he said, hardly recognizing the gritty sound of his own voice.

"Bram?" Glory said dreamily. "What…what's wrong?"

"This is wrong. I said that making love wasn't to be a part of our pretend marriage. It was a promise I made to you so you wouldn't have to be afraid of me in any way. I'm *not* going to seduce you into bed."

Glory blinked, attempting to focus her sense of reality and reason.

"But you want me, don't you?" she said.

"Hell, yes, I want you, but—"

"*You* decided we weren't to make love. *You* dictated those terms, just as I did about the rigid budget. We didn't discuss the issue of making love, Bram.''

"But—"

"I want you as much as you want me. I have the right to say that, to express my desire for you. Make love with me, Bram. Please."

And with that simple plea Bram Bishop was lost.

With a groan that rumbled from deep in his chest, he kissed Glory, then lifted his head and swung her up into his arms. He strode down the hall to her bedroom, set her on her feet, then swept back the linens on the bed to reveal mint green sheets.

"Glory," he said, framing her face with his hands, "are you sure? No regrets? I couldn't handle it if—"

"I'm sure," she said softly. "No regrets."

"Your hair," he said. "Would you take down your hair?"

A gentle smile touched Glory's lips as her hands floated upward to pull the pins from her hair.

Why? a tiny voice in her mind nudged, as she dropped the pins haphazardly to the floor. Why was she about to make love with a man she was still convinced had been set on seduction from the moment they'd met? Why in heaven's name was she doing this?

Because…because she wanted to.

Because for once in her life she was going to let go, not analyze, not be clinical or professional or textbook perfect. She just wanted to feel.

Because she desired Bram with an intensity like nothing she'd ever known before.

Because Bram was beautiful and sensitive and so magnificently male.

Because Bram Bishop knew how to love, having been surrounded by love his entire life.

Because she genuinely cared for him, and for these two weeks, stolen out of time, she was his wife.

Glory shook her head, then fluttered her fingers through her hair to untangle it. It tumbled to the middle of her back in a silky, strawberry blond cascade.

"Oh, Lord," Bram said, hardly able to breathe. "Your hair is so beautiful, *you're* so beautiful." He reached out one hand to sift his fingers through the silken strands. "Incredible."

"Thank you."

Then Glory began to remove her clothes. She looked directly into Bram's eyes, now smoky blue with desire, lifted her chin and disrobed, standing naked and womanly and proud before him.

An achy sensation closed Bram's throat, making it impossible for him to speak. He trailed one thumb over Glory's lips, trying, hoping somehow to convey that he understood that she was giving him her greatest gift...the essence of herself, her trust, her caring.

Bram quickly shed his clothes, knowing he had *never* desired a woman as much as he did Glory Carson. But he also realized that new, strange and wondrous emotions were present, rising to the fore, intermingling with his physical want.

Glory's heated gaze swept over Bram, savoring all that she saw, etching each detail indelibly in her mind.

Yes, he truly was magnificent.

Bram placed Glory in the center of the bed, then

followed her down, covering her mouth with his in the process. He stretched out next to her, keeping his weight on one forearm as he splayed a hand on her flat stomach, then moved upward to stroke the nipple of one breast with his thumb.

A soft purr of pleasure whispered from her throat. Her hands roamed over Bram's back, savoring the feel of the taut muscles bunching beneath her palms. The heat deep within her burned hotter, licking flames consuming her with passion.

They kissed, caressed, discovered the wondrous mysteries of each other's body, awed by the differences. What they found became theirs to cherish, revere, rejoice in.

Time lost meaning. Desire soared to heights before unknown, but by unspoken agreement they held back, anticipating the moment when they would become one entity.

"Bram, please," Glory whispered finally, her voice a near sob.

"Yes," he murmured, his lips skimming over the dewy skin of her stomach.

He moved above her, sapphire blue eyes meeting those of emerald green. His muscles quivered with forced restraint as he entered her, the welcoming, moist heat of her femininity receiving all of him.

The tempo Bram set was slow as he watched Glory's face for any sign that he was hurting her with his size and strength. She lifted her hips, and he increased the cadence, Glory matching him in perfect synchronization.

They danced the dance of lovers, as old as forever,

new and theirs alone. The rhythm became a pounding, thundering beat, carrying them up and away...so far, far away, hurling them at last, *at last,* over the abyss into an oblivion of ecstasy.

"Bram!"

"Ah, Glory!"

They hovered, holding fast to each other, returning slowly to the room, the bed, the mint green sheets, reality.

Bram collapsed, his strength spent. He rolled onto his back to keep from crushing the exquisite, delicate woman beneath him, but kept her close to his side.

Glory, his mind hummed, in sated contentment. She was no longer Chicago Glory, she was Texas Glory. She was his.

"Wonderful," he said quietly. "You were...we were...together...wonderful."

"Yes," Glory said, weaving her fingers through the moist curls on his chest. "Oh, yes, Bram. Wonderful."

"No regrets?"

"No."

Several minutes passed in comfortable, lovely silence, then Glory laughed softly.

"Hmm?" Bram said.

"I just remembered what the sixth most common reason is for divorce."

"What is it?"

"Uninspired sex."

Bram chuckled. Glory savored the oh-so-masculine sound.

"I do believe, ma'am," Bram said, "that we're in no danger from number six."

"I do believe, sir, that you're right."

Silence fell again, then sleep claimed them, their heads resting on the same pillow. Several hours later they woke, reaching for each other, giving, receiving, holding nothing back.

They soared again. Returned again. Slept again.

"Glory?" Bram said at some point in the long night of lovemaking.

"Yes?"

"We never had our pizza."

"Tomorrow."

"Yeah, tomorrow. There are endless tomorrows."

Glory frowned slightly in the darkness.

Endless tomorrows? she thought sleepily. No, that wasn't true. They had two weeks. Two weeks to be together, to be husband and wife, to laugh, talk, share, make love.

She knew that and so did Bram. Didn't he? Yes, of course, he did. Don't think, Glory Carson. Just be.

She snuggled closer to Bram and gave way to blissful slumber.

Early the next morning Bram stood in the kitchen, staring out the window above the sink as he sipped from a mug of hot coffee.

He usually cooked himself a hearty breakfast before heading to work, but there was such a tight knot of tension in his stomach that he knew he couldn't eat a bite.

He was suffering, he realized incredulously, from a giant-size case of the morning-after jitters. If he'd ever been a victim of this malady in the past, it was so long ago he didn't remember.

What was Glory thinking regarding their hours of lovemaking the previous night? In the light of the new day, was she having the regrets she'd been so certain wouldn't surface?

Or was she smiling, feeling a buzz of happiness that matched the one he'd had upon first awakening?

He'd heard the shower start as he entered the kitchen, and he knew enough time had passed that Glory should be appearing any moment.

Man, he was a wreck.

The night shared with Glory, the lovemaking, the physical and emotional connecting, was like nothing he'd experienced before. It was all so new, rich, deep and *very* special.

Something important was happening between him and Glory Carson, and he had every intention of discovering exactly what it was.

"Bram?"

He spun around so fast at the sound of Glory's voice that he nearly spilled his coffee.

Glory Carson, the psychologist, was back, he thought instantly. Hair twisted up behind her head. Dark blue slacks, pale pink blouse, navy blazer. And Dr. Carson wasn't smiling.

"Good morning," Bram said, forcing a lightness to his voice. "Are you hungry? I'll be glad to fry you a couple of eggs."

"No, thank you. I only have coffee and yogurt for breakfast."

Bram crossed the room to sit down at the table.

Glory joined him minutes later with a mug of coffee and a small container of yogurt.

"Is everything all right?" Bram asked, looking at her intently.

Glory took a sip of coffee, then met his gaze. "I hope so, Bram."

"What does that mean? Don't you know if everything is all right, Glory? How do you feel about what we shared last night?"

"It was wonderful," she said smiling. "Exquisitely beautiful."

The knot in Bram's stomach began to untwist.

"But..." Glory went on.

The knot retightened.

"But?" he echoed.

Glory sighed, no trace of her smile remaining. "Bram, at some point last night you said that we have endless tomorrows. You might not even recall saying it. If so, there's no reason to discuss it."

Bram frowned. "I most definitely remember saying it, and it's true. This is one of those tomorrows right here." He swept one hand through the air. "We're living it. Together."

"That's correct, but the tomorrows we're to share aren't endless, they're numbered. We have a total of two weeks, several days of which are already gone."

"Oh, now wait a minute..."

Glory raised one hand. "Please, listen to me. I do *not* regret our making love. We're both adults who are free to make that momentous, mutually agreed upon decision.

"But, Bram, it doesn't change who I am, what I

believe. We want different things in the future. You wish to marry, have a wife and children. I never intend to engage in that life-style. As long as all that is still clearly understood, then, yes, everything is all right.''

Bram flattened his hands on the table and leaned back in the chair, staring at Glory.

"You're engaging in a two-week fling?" he said, narrowing his eyes. "A wham-bam affair, then I'm out on my butt?"

"We agreed on a two-week timetable," she said, her voice rising. "Don't you dare make this sound cheap or tacky. You're in your husband-to-be boot camp mode, and I'm gathering research for prenuptial counseling. Nothing has changed from that agenda.''

Bram shoved his chair back, got to his feet and crossed the room. He gripped the edge of the sink as he stared unseeing out the window.

Damn it, his mind roared. He couldn't believe this. He hadn't made a dent in Glory's wall, not one little chip had fallen away. It was as though last night had never taken place.

Easy, Bishop, don't lose your cool.

Last night was a reality, it had happened, and Glory couldn't erase it, any of it. They had not only made love, they'd made memories, and he was counting on the fact that they wouldn't be all that easily dismissed from her mind. But her heart?

Glory watched Bram, saw the tight set of his muscled body, could feel the tension emanating from him like a nearly palpable entity.

This was confusing, she thought, frowning. If Bram had been set on seduction as she believed, then he had achieved his goal. Why was he obviously battling a fit of anger?

Well, there was the issue of her never wishing to marry that had created the double challenge. And, she imagined, Bram didn't care for being lectured to first thing in the morning on the rules of the game.

Rules of the *game?*

No, that was a poor choice of word. She wasn't engaged in a sexual game. She'd never stoop so low. The *plan* was sound and would benefit her a great deal on a professional level.

Her decision to make love with Bram Bishop was separate from the ultimate benefits to be reaped from this two weeks.

There. *She* was all right. *She* was fine. What happened next depended on what Bram said and did when he spoke again. If he didn't break the sink apart with his bare hands in the meantime!

Bram turned from the sink, no readable expression on his face.

"You're absolutely on the money, Glory," he said. "I got off the track there for a bit. Chalk it up to sexual afterglow, or whatever. Two weeks, it is, then you go your way, and I graduate from boot camp and go mine.

"It's not tacky, it's what we originally agreed upon. No problem. In less than two weeks, I'll be out of your life."

"Oh," Glory said. Why did she feel as though the temperature in the room had just dropped about twenty degrees? Why was she suddenly so cold, so hollow feeling? Oh, Glory, stop it. Drink your coffee. "Well, good. I'm glad we discussed this."

Bram walked slowly back to the table, but didn't sit down.

"You bet," he said. "This communication business is great stuff, once you get the hang of it." He paused. "Well, I have to hit the road. Let's see...tonight. How's this? I'll pick you up here after work and we'll go out for the ever-famous pizza, then over to my place."

"Yes, that's fine."

"Okay, wife, I'm leaving for work now."

"'Bye."

"Glory, Glory," Bram said, shaking his head. "Leaving with appropriate behavior is just as important as the welcome home."

"Oh," she said, getting quickly to her feet. "I'll walk you to the door."

"That won't be necessary," he said, encircling her with his arms. "You can send me off with a proper goodbye while in the kitchen."

"Well, I—"

"Shh."

Bram claimed her mouth in a kiss that was so searing, so intense, that Glory had to cling to his biceps for support. He finally released her, set her back down on the chair, then moved her coffee mug directly in front of her.

"Have a good day," he said.

Bram strode from the room, whistling a peppy tune as he left the house.

"You have a good day—" Glory drew a steadying breath "—too."

*   *   *

Bram stopped whistling as soon as he closed the front door behind him. As he drove away from the house, a muscle ticked in his tightly clenched jaw.

Glory Carson had just declared war, he fumed.

She was calling all the shots again, rapping him on the knuckles and reminding him of how things stood between them. She was well and truly entrenched behind that damnable wall of hers.

Well, Dr. Carson was forgetting a very important fact.

He was Bram Bishop of Bishop Construction. He was a pro at building structures.

He was also very adept at tearing them down....

Seven

Glory looked up to see her secretary, Margot, stand-ing in the doorway.

"I just wanted to say good-night," Margot said.

Glory smiled. "Have a nice evening."

Margot walked slowly forward, a thoughtful ex-pression on her face.

"I realized this afternoon that you haven't men-tioned that handsome Bram Bishop since you went out with him for a dinner meeting. Did you agree to his plan for 'prenuptial training'? I believe that is the term that was used."

Glory felt an instant flush of heat stain her cheeks as images of the lovemaking shared with Bram flashed before her mental vision.

"Yes," she said, getting to her feet, "as a matter

of fact the program is in full operation. I can already see that it's going to be very beneficial to my clients.

"For example, I've learned that I've been much too hasty in urging couples to adhere to a strict budget to hopefully avoid quarrels about money.

"There has to be a bit of 'give,' with some funds set aside for fun, like going out for pizza, or ordering it in if they're too weary to leave the house again after coming home from work."

"Interesting," Margot said.

"Oh, and that's another thing. I must add the importance of the appropriate attention being given to their separating in the morning, then greeting each other again when they return home. People should feel special in their own home as often as is possible because... Why are you smiling like that, Margot?"

"Me?" she said, raising her eyebrows. "Well, it's just very nice to see you so excited about something. Your eyes are actually sparkling."

"Yes, well," Glory said, smoothing the lapels of her blazer, "any professional psychologist would be pleased upon gaining new insights into their specialty. Once I have all my research gathered from this study with Bram, I'll structure a prenuptial counseling course, then begin the process of advertising it."

"Mmm," Margot said, nodding. "The sparkling eyes have nothing to do with Bram Bishop, himself, then?"

"Don't be silly, Margot," she said, moving from behind the desk. "Bram and I agreed on a two-week boot camp, to use his phrase. After that I'll never see him again. We'll each have what we hoped to gain from the plan and will go our separate ways. And that's...fine, just fine.''

"Glory Carson, I've been a mother for more years than you've been on this earth. I know when I'm being conned. However, in this case I do believe you're not being completely honest with *yourself*.''

Glory frowned as she looked at the older woman.

"What on earth do you mean, Margot? I'm sincerely pleased with the information that I'm—''

"Oh, honey,'' Margot interrupted, "at the very moment you spoke of not seeing Bram Bishop again, the sparkle disappeared from your pretty eyes. It was like a cloud moving over the sun. I do hope you're keeping in touch with your inner feelings, the way you advise your clients to.'' She paused. "I must dash, or I'll miss my bus. Good night, Glory.''

"Good night, Margot,'' she said quietly.

The silence that ensued when Margot left the office felt like a heavy, uncomfortable blanket falling over Glory.

"I *am* keeping in touch with myself,'' she said aloud.

Glory wrapped her hands around her elbows in a protective gesture as her own words seemed to hurl back at her, taunting her. She sank onto one of the chairs in front of the desk.

All right, she admitted, she'd had a difficult time concentrating today due to recurring memories of the exquisitely beautiful lovemaking shared with Bram.

She had seen him so clearly in her mind's eye, could hear that rumbly, sexy chuckle, smell his aroma of soap and man, recall vividly the feel of his magnificent body.

Okay, the emergence of Bram into her life had had a tremendous impact on her. She was alive, wasn't she? She was a woman, wasn't she? She'd have to be a corpse not to be stirred by a man such as Bram.

And, yes, she cared for and about Bram, wanted him to be happy, find what he was seeking in life. Bram Bishop mattered to her, but that was reasonable, because she was a compassionate person.

Had her eyes "ceased to sparkle" when she'd spoken of Bram's walking away, never to be seen again? Margot was being fanciful, reading too many romance novels, or watching gooey movies too often. When Bram was gone, he'd be gone. End of story. No big deal.

Glory sighed.

Okay, so she'd miss him…a little…for a few days…and nights. That was perfectly natural, for Pete's sake, because she would have lived with the man for two weeks as his wife.

Wife.

Mrs. Bram Bishop.

Glory Carson Bishop.

"Stop it this instant, Glory Carson," she said, jumping to her feet.

She refused to regret the decision to become Bram's wife in the physical sense while they were together. Their lovemaking was a gift she was giving to herself to treasure, cherish, to create beautiful memories that would be hers to keep for all time.

No one would be hurt by what she and Bram were doing. *No one.*

Keep in touch with herself? She was. She definitely was. She knew who she was, what she was doing and why she was doing it.

There were no risks involved here, because she would not allow herself to fall in love with Bram. That foolish mistake would be the only reason she would cry tears of heartbreak and loneliness when he was gone.

And that emotional error simply wasn't going to happen.

"Oh-h-h, I'm so stuffed I'm going to pop," Glory said with a moan and a smile. "That was the most delicious pizza I've ever had. Thank you, Bram."

Bram matched her smile. "You're very welcome. I'm glad you enjoyed it."

Glory glanced around the large room. "This restaurant is such fun. Definitely noisy, but fun. The idea of having the waiters and waitresses zooming back and forth on roller skates is so clever. And the oldies-but-goodies music and... Well, it's a hit, as evidenced by the number of people in here. How did you ever find this place?"

"I built it."

"Really?"

"Yep. You're looking at a Bishop Construction creation. The floor was a killer. We had a heck of a time finding the wood to make it, and to be able to guarantee it would hold up. You don't buy roller derby supplies at every lumberyard on the block."

Glory nodded slowly. "I think I envy you." She paused. "Yes, I know I do."

"Why?"

"Because you have tangible, visible evidence of your chosen career, your life's work. You started from nothing and—" she swept one hand through the air "—now here it is, being enjoyed. That must be very rewarding."

"It is. Each project I bid on is a new challenge, and no two days are the same in the construction business. You have to be prepared for anything at any time." Bram frowned slightly. "But your career is rewarding, too, isn't it?"

"Yes, but in a different way. *I* have to reassure myself that I'm making a contribution and helping people. Couples who seek marriage counseling don't circle back a year or so later to inform me they're still on the right track or thank me for what I did."

"Why don't they?"

"Because I'm a reminder of darker times, the stormy weather in their relationship. I turn them loose and cross my fingers. I rarely know how it all ended up for them." Glory laughed. "I'd make a great mother bird. I'm an expert at pushing my charges out of the nest."

"You'd make a wonderful mother...period," Bram said, looking directly at her. "You care very deeply about whatever it is you're doing, and you give it your maximum effort and attention. The child who would be the recipient of your motherly love would be very fortunate."

"Thank you, Bram," Glory said softly. "That was a lovely thing to say."

"Well, I mean it. I also believe that your husband, the father of that child, would be a helluva lucky guy, too."

"I..." Glory started, then stopped speaking.

She didn't know what to say, she realized. Another *thank you* was too breezy, too lightweight for the tremendous compliments Bram was paying her.

She'd be a wonderful wife and mother? She'd never given it much thought, due to the fact that she didn't plan to take those roles. Growing up in the war zone with her parents had etched that decision in stone.

But Bram meant what he was saying. Sincerity was evident in his voice, in the expression on his face, in the depths of his beautiful blue eyes. Yes, he truly believed what he'd just said.

What she didn't understand was why Bram's words were filling her with such a gentle warmth, a soft glow, that she wanted to hold fast to, savor and treasure as a precious gift.

So why was she, a dedicated career woman, with no room, *no desire*, to have a husband and children in her life, tucking away Bram's declarations in a special, private chamber of her heart?

She didn't *know* why, and the confusion that mystery was creating in her mind was very disturbing.

"Hey," Bram said, rapping his knuckles on the wooden table. "Anybody home? You look like I just told you that you'd be a terrific candidate for a root canal."

"What? Oh, I'm sorry. I was off on a mental tangent somewhere.'' Glory produced a small smile. ''My brain is on pizza overload.''

Glory's brain, Bram thought, was hopefully digesting what he'd just told her. Because, oh, yes, Glory Carson would be a wonderful mother and, yes, she was most definitely a wife candidate. No, correct that...a candidate to be *his* wife.

''Are you ready to leave this noisy place and go to my apartment?'' he asked.

''Yes, that's fine.''

''You know, in order for this to have a feel of reality, you'll have to waltz into my apartment as though you do it every evening. We went out for pizza and are now going home. Since we're married, that wouldn't include a tour of the adobe.''

''Good point,'' Glory said, nodding. ''I'll wing it. Ignore me if I walk into a closet, instead of into the bathroom.''

Bram chuckled. ''Oh, okay.'' He frowned in the next moment. ''We have a lot of the evening left to kick back and relax. You're still in your work clothes.''

''Here we go again,'' Glory said, rolling her eyes heavenward. ''What is it with you and my clothes, Bram?''

''I don't know.'' He lifted one shoulder in a shrug. ''You just seem so...so stiff, so still in your professional mode, because you don't change into something more comfortable.''

''The clothes I wear to the office *are* comfortable. Sometimes I change into something else when I get home, other times I don't.''

"What, for example, would you put on?"

"My robe, if it's raining and chilly. Shorts or maybe a loose sundress if it's particularly hot and sticky."

"Not jeans?"

Glory leaned toward him. "No, because I don't own a pair of jeans."

"Shh," Bram said. "Don't say that so loud, or they'll ask you to leave town. You're not allowed to live in Houston, Texas, ma'am, and not own a pair of jeans. It's against the law."

"Well, partner," she said, laughing, "ol' Chicago Glory here is going to get arrested, I guess."

"You're Texas Glory now," Bram said, his smile fading into a serious expression. "You live here, belong here." *With me.* "I think we should go shopping and buy you some jeans."

"Whoa," Glory said, holding up one hand. "Slow down. Are you attempting to change me into something—someone—you want me to be? That's a major problem in a great many marriages, Bram."

Bram stared into space for a long moment, then looked at Glory again.

"Okay," he said. "Try this. My brother Blue owns a ranch, the Rocking B. If we made plans to go out there to visit Blue and Amy, what would you wear?"

"To a ranch, an honest-to-goodness Texas ranch? Horses, cows, pigs and whatever?"

"Yep."

"Well, I guess I'd want to see everything, maybe even try riding a horse for the first time in my life. So, I'd need the proper apparel, such as a pair of jeans."

"Bingo. I don't feel that falls under the ominous category of trying to change you. You're simply adapting to your new extended family. Let's go shopping."

"Have I been conned?"

"By me?" Bram said, getting to his feet. "Don't be silly. Oh, I'll buy you a trench coat, fedora and sunglasses, too."

"Whatever for?" she said, rising to stand next to him.

"My other brother, Tux," he said, laughing, "is a private investigator. You'll need that outfit when we visit him and Nancy."

"You," Glory said, smiling, "are cuckoo."

"Yeah," he said, wrapping one arm around her shoulders. "But I'm lovable. Let's hit the road and find the nearest mall."

Yes, Glory thought, as they left the restaurant, Bram *was* lovable. That was a fact, a dangerous detail. She, however, was *not* going to fall in love with lovable Bram Bishop.

The shopping spree was fun.

Glory could not remember when she'd felt so carefree, young and happy. She'd decided to just "go with the flow" regarding Bram's insistence that she own a pair of jeans.

She laughed until she had to wrap her arms around her stomach as Bram peered in the windows of three stores, rejected them, then took Glory's hand and pulled her toward the fourth.

Once satisfied with the available selection, Bram

held up various colors and styles of jeans in front of Glory, as a saleswoman hovered in the background.

"Okay," Bram said finally. "Here are three different pairs to try on. There's a boot cut, straight leg, and this one has buttons instead of a zipper. If none of these work, I'll keep hunting."

"Yes, sir." Another bubble of laughter escaped from Glory.

"Do you own a Western shirt?" Bram said.

"No."

"My work is never done." He shook his head. "I'll pick out some for you to try on."

"Bram," Glory whispered, "this store is a bit expensive for my clothing budget. One pair of jeans is all I can manage."

Bram gripped her shoulders. "*I'm* buying my wife some clothes. The budget definitely includes a shirt to go with the jeans."

As Glory opened her mouth to protest, Bram dropped a quick kiss on her lips.

"Please, Glory, let me do this. It would give me a great deal of pleasure, and it *was* my idea. As my wife, don't you think you should graciously accept what I sincerely would like you to have?"

"Well, if you put it that way..."

"Good." He brushed his lips over hers again. "Thank you very much."

Their eyes met, along with matching warm smiles. Bram cleared his throat and turned Glory toward the fitting rooms.

"Go," he said. "I'll sit in that chair over there and wait for the fashion show."

In the small room, Glory wiggled into a pair of jeans, then slid her hands down her hips.

These jeans had better not shrink, she thought. She'd never worn anything so formfitting. But she had to admit she didn't look so bad.

"Excuse me," the saleswoman said, knocking on the louvered door.

Glory opened the door. "Yes?"

"Your husband said he would like you to try on this shirt. He's certain—oh, my, he's absolutely right—he said it was the exact same shade of green as your eyes." The woman smiled. "After thirty years, I doubt seriously if my husband even remembers what color my eyes are. Are you two newlyweds?"

"Well," Glory said slowly, "we haven't been husband and wife for very long."

"It shows. I could tell from the way you look at each other that you're very much in love. It's delightful to see. Try on this shirt with the jeans, dear. Those pants certainly fit you perfectly."

Glory accepted the shirt and closed the door.

I could tell from the way you look at each other that you're very much in love.

Glory stood statue still, staring at her reflection in the full-length mirror, as the saleswoman's words echoed in her mind.

That was nonsense, she thought. The woman had seen what she *wished* to see. She and Bram weren't exchanging loving gazes. They simply looked at each other once in a while as they were talking.

She leaned closer to the mirror and examined her face.

Her cheeks were a bit flushed. Her eyes were crystal clear, bright, almost sparkling.

Oh, Glory, stop, she told herself. Try on the shirt and forget what that woman said.

Refusing to think about the woman's comments and perhaps ruin the enjoyment of the outing with Bram, Glory snapped the Western shirt closed. She tucked the tail in the jeans, then bloused it over the waistband to conceal the absence of a belt.

Pleased with what she saw in the mirror, she unpinned her hair, allowing the single braid to hang down her back. Deciding her low-heeled pumps were too dressy for the leisure-time outfit, she padded barefoot out of the fitting room to find Bram.

"Ta-da," she said, when she was ten feet in front of the chair where Bram was sitting. "I hereby present...Texas Glory." She floated her arms away from her sides in a graceful motion, then turned slowly around for Bram's inspection. "What do you think?"

Bram's gaze was riveted on Glory, and his heart was beating so wildly he could hear the echo of its rapid tempo in his ears.

What did he think? he mentally repeated, getting to his feet.

He thought Glory was the most beautiful woman he'd ever seen.

He thought she looked spectacular in casual clothes—*Texas* clothes. He could picture her, with no stretch of his imagination, wearing those jeans as she played with her children. *Their* children.

He thought—no, he *knew*—that inch by emotional inch, he was falling in love with Glory Carson.

Bram went to where Glory stood smiling at him, framed her face in his hands and kissed her deeply.

"Oh, my goodness," the saleswoman said with a wistful sigh. "That is the sweetest, most romantic thing I've ever seen."

Bram lifted his head, suddenly remembering where he was. Glory blushed a pretty pink.

"We'll take the shirt and jeans," Bram said to the saleswoman. "Plus she needs socks and tennis shoes."

"Certainly," the woman said. "I assume your wife will be wearing her new outfit?"

Bram looked directly into Glory's eyes. "Yes, my wife will stay in these clothes. Would you pack her other things, please?"

"Of course." The woman hurried away.

"Thank you, Bram," Glory said. "This is a very lovely gift."

"You're welcome, Mrs. Bishop." He paused. "By the way, you look beautiful."

Glory laughed. "I *feel* beautiful. I'm wearing jeans, for heaven's sake, and I feel beautiful." She shrugged. "Go figure."

"Well, I'd say," Bram said, "that you've just discovered a part of you that you didn't realize was there. I can't help but wonder what else you might yet find out about yourself."

Before Glory could reply, the saleswoman returned with a stack of boxes containing tennis shoes for Glory to try on.

Glory's lighthearted mood remained firmly in place as they drove toward Bram's apartment. In his enormous living room, she swept her gaze over the large, masculine-appearing furniture.

"It suits you," she said, nodding.

"Shh," he said, smiling. "You live here, remember? You wouldn't suddenly be commenting on the furniture."

Glory laughed. "I think I'd better pretend one of my flowery chairs is plunked in here. This is a very masculine decor, just as my cottage is done in feminine frills."

Bram wrapped his arms around Glory and nestled her to him.

"We'll compromise, blend the two together, make it work for both of us."

"Excellent," she said. "People are marrying at an older age now, compared to the past. It stands to reason they'd each have material things. It wouldn't be fair for one of them to be expected to give up all that they own."

"Of course not." Bram kissed her quickly, then trailed a ribbon of kisses along her slender throat. "There will be some of you, some of me, joined into one entity that is sensational."

Were they still talking about furniture? Glory wondered hazily, as heated desire consumed her.

"Handy things, these Western shirts," Bram said, unsnapping Glory's.

"Very efficient," she said, doing the same to Bram's shirt. "Snaps are nice."

Glory splayed her fingers on Bram's chest, savoring the feel of the springy, curly hair and the hard muscles beneath his tanned skin.

A groan rumbled from Bram's throat, as he freed Glory's shirt from the jeans, unsnapped the cuffs, then drew it away to drop it to the floor.

"You'll wrinkle my new shirt," she said.

"I'll buy you another one."

"These jeans are so tight, I'm not sure they'll come off."

Bram chuckled as he swung her up into his arms.

"Due to the vast population of the state of Texas," he said, striding toward the hallway leading to his bedroom, "I think it's a safe bet to say that even the tightest jeans can be removed."

"Do tell."

"*Show* and tell, Glory. It's much more effective."

They made love in Bram's king-size bed. Exquisite love. Love that was new, yet wondrously familiar at the same time. They touched, kissed, hands never still, lips following where hands had gone.

Bodies glistened, hearts beat in thundering tempos, heat suffused them with licking flames of passion.

As Bram drew the soft bounty of one of Glory's breasts deep into his mouth, she closed her eyes to savor the tantalizing sensations sweeping through her.

"Oh, Bram," she whispered.

He paid homage to her other breast, drinking of her sweetness, his aroused body aching for release.

Glory splayed her hands flat on Bram's back, pressing him close, never wishing to let him go.

The coiled, hot tension within them increased to the point of near pain.

"Glory?"

"Yes. Please, Bram. Now."

He moved over her and into her, thrusting deep, filling her. She received all that he brought to the moist darkness of her femininity.

And they danced *their* dance. Only theirs. Harder. Faster. Flinging them up and over the edge of reality. It was ecstasy. They hovered there, returned slowly, drifting down, holding fast to each other, then rested in sated contentment.

"Glory," Bram said, much later.

"Hmm?" she murmured, as she lay snuggled close to his side. "Yes?"

"You still haven't told me all the things on that list of reasons for divorce."

"Oh." She yawned sleepily. "Well, there are two that I don't think would ever happen to you, Bram. If your wife believed in and worked at the forever love you've spoken of, you'd never have to deal with them."

"What are they?"

"Number five is falling out of love. The emotion of love just isn't there anymore. Number nine is when one of the partners in the marriage falls in love with someone else. They almost sound like the same thing, but they're really not."

"No, I realize that."

"But if you discover your forever love, you'll be very happy for...well, forever. I sincerely hope you *do* find it, Bram."

I have, he thought. Oh, yes, he was holding his forever love in his arms at that very moment.

He was in love with Glory.

Bram looked at her, saw her lashes drifting down

as sleep claimed her. He rested his lips lightly on her forehead, a frown knitting his brow.

Damn it, he fumed, why had he mentioned that crummy list? Everything had been so perfect, the entire evening fantastic, until he'd opened his big mouth.

Then Glory had changed, sounding like Dr. Carson, psychologist and marriage counselor. It was as though he'd been sitting in the chair opposite the desk in her office, hearing her wishing him success in finding the woman who would be his forever love.

Didn't Glory consider even for a moment that that woman was her?

Hadn't he made the least bit of progress at chipping away at her damnable protective wall?

Eight

During the night Bram was awake more than asleep. He conducted an ongoing argument with himself regarding the subject of sitting Glory down and telling her that he wanted to *really* discover what they might have together, no longer having her play a role for research.

As for himself, he would explain that all he had done and said since becoming her husband had been the real goods, not a performance, just Bram Bishop being Bram Bishop.

But wait, his mind hollered in return. If Glory was pressured, pushed in any way, she would probably cancel the program and send him packing.

Glory had made up her mind many years before to never marry. He was fighting the ghosts and memories of her youth, which were proving to be mighty foes.

The wall around her heart was solidly and depressingly in place.

He'd better not rock the boat, he decided, close to dawn. He'd use every minute of the remaining days...and nights...in the agreed-upon two weeks, to *show* Glory that something special and important was happening between them.

He didn't dare, at this point, tell her that he loved her, declare her to be his forever love and ask her to marry him.

With a sigh Bram dozed off once again.

Glory opened her eyes, then sat bolt upright on the bed an instant later, looking frantically for the clock that was on the nightstand.

"Oh, no," she said. "Look at the time." She threw back the blankets, left the bed and began to snatch her clothes from the floor. "Bram, wake up. We're late."

"What? What?" Bram said, struggling to sit up.

"See what time it is? I've got to shower, dress, go home, put on fresh clothes, then get to the office. I'll never make it on time. I can't believe this. I've never been late for an appointment with a client."

"Calm down, Glory," Bram said.

"I don't have time to calm down!"

She dashed into the bathroom and slammed the door behind her.

"Great way to start the day," Bram muttered, swinging his feet to the floor.

And it got worse.

Glory kept after Bram to hurry. He said he was moving as fast as he could. He started a pot of coffee brewing, only to have Glory state she couldn't spare one second for a cup. Bram said if they were already late, what difference would another ten minutes make? Glory shot him a look that resulted in him raising both hands in a gesture of peace and silently vowing not to say another word.

At Glory's house, she opened the door to the Blazer as soon as Bram pulled into the driveway and pressed on the brake.

"'Bye," she said.

"Hey, wait a second," Bram said. "What kind of send-off is that?"

"There's no time for playing games, Bram."

He reached across the seat, gripped her shoulders, turned her toward him and kissed her deeply.

"This isn't a game," he said. "There's always time for an appropriate goodbye. Have a nice day. I'll pick you up here right after work. We've having dinner at my parents' house."

"Since when?"

"Since I saw it written on my calendar while you were zooming around the apartment."

"You might have told me."

"I just did! It's not a big deal. It's only dinner-at-the-folks' night. We do it on a regular basis."

"I can't barge in on a family gathering. You go and I'll stay home."

"Damn it, Glory, you're my wife. I wouldn't go to my parents' house for dinner and leave you behind."

"I don't have time to discuss this."

"Good. Then it's settled. I'll pick you up here and we'll go."

"Whatever," she said, definitely sounding cross. "Goodbye, Bram."

She slid off the seat, closed the door and ran across the lawn to the house.

"And I repeat," Bram said, putting the Blazer in reverse, "this is a great way to start the day." He paused. "Hell."

The stressful beginning of the day had produced a headache that pounded in Glory's temples and refused to budge.

By the time she drove home she was exhausted and wanted nothing more than a light dinner and a quiet evening. The prospect of meeting Bram's family for the first time held no appeal whatsoever.

Two blocks from her cottage, she decided she'd simply inform Bram that she wasn't up to going and bid him adieu. It really didn't make any difference if she attended the informal gathering, anyway.

Glory frowned.

Or did it?

As Bram's *wife* she most certainly should make the effort to join him at his family home for dinner. It would be self-centered to refuse to go because she was tired and had a nagging headache.

She was no longer a single entity, whose actions affected no one but herself. She was a married woman, who should reach deeper for energy and patience on her husband's behalf.

She and Bram should compromise. She'd agree to go to dinner despite her fatigue. He'd agree to make it an early evening.

That was the way it *should* be done. What remained to be seen was if Bram was open to the idea of leaving his parents' house shortly after finishing the meal.

A dollar bet, Glory thought, narrowing her eyes, said that Bram would pitch a fit.

In a mood that was less than sunny, Glory parked next to Bram's vehicle in her driveway, then marched across the stepping stones to the house. She entered the living room, and Bram got to his feet from where he was sitting on the sofa.

"Bram—"

"Glory—"

They'd both spoken, then stopped, at the same time.

"You first," Bram said.

"Yes, well, I just wanted to say that I'm very tired and have a killer headache. I'm willing to go to your parents' house for dinner, but I insist...no, wait...I'd appreciate it if we came home early."

"Oh."

Gear up, Glory, she told herself. Bram was about to erupt in a screamer, no doubt about it.

"Well," he said, "*I* was going to say that it wasn't fair of me to drop the bulletin of this outing on you with no warning. I was going to offer to call and cancel. My folks will understand, and I certainly would, too."

Glory stared at Bram as though she'd never seen him before in her life.

"You'd...you'd do that for me?" she said finally.

Bram nodded. "Yes, I would. I figured you'd had a generally lousy day, because the way it started was upsetting for you. You know, you like order, not chaos. Dumping this dinner deal on you was probably the last straw." He shrugged. "So, we won't go."

"No, no, it's all right. We'll compromise. I wouldn't want to be the cause of your family being disappointed that they didn't see you as planned." Glory paused. "You're working very hard at being a good husband, aren't you?"

"Yes, of course, I am. I'm not treating these two weeks lightly, believe me." Bram looked at her intently. "*You're* giving your role as my wife maximum effort, aren't you?"

Glory frowned slightly. "Yes, I guess I am, now that I think about it."

"Good, that's good. Shall we go?"

Glory's fatigue and headache were forgotten within minutes of entering the senior Bishops' home. She was welcomed with warm, friendly smiles, and was soon laughing at the ongoing banter taking place among the three brothers.

Amy and Nancy Bishop were the type of women who made a person feel she had known them for years. Glory asked Nancy how the huge toy panda was adjusting to its new home, which led to the hilarious story of how Glory and Bram had met.

Jana-John and Abe Bishop made Glory feel so special with their smiles and an indefinable "something" that emanated sincere caring.

Jana-John was lovely and had an almost ethereal aura, as she seemed to float with a natural gracefulness.

Abe was tall, thin and a bit disheveled, his keen

blue eyes darting from one person to the next with intense interest.

The menu for the meal was a bit unusual, but everyone took it in stride. Her muse, Jana-John stated, was having a potato day. So dinner consisted of an enormous potato salad served with crusty rolls. She'd even painted a picture of potatoes with human features, which had been marvelous fun.

When Bram began to explain the "husband boot camp" program, Glory felt her cheeks flush with embarrassment. But as she glanced quickly around the table, she saw no hint of knowing smiles or wicked winks that indicated the Bishops thought training to be a husband meant making love with one's wife. The family appeared to be receiving the information with serious attention.

"Interesting," Tux said, giving no indication he'd known previously of the plan.

"Isn't it, though?" Blue said, all innocence. "So, how's it coming along? Are you ready to throw Bram out, Glory?"

She smiled. "No. We've had our tense moments regarding the budget and leaving shoes on the living room floor, but we've compromised on many issues. The research I'm gathering for my prenuptial counseling is invaluable."

"Back in history," Abe said, using the phrase his sons had heard all of their lives, "many countries began training girls to be proper wives from the time the little ones were walking and talking."

"Sounds good to me," Tux said.

"That was then," Nancy said, "and this is now, husband dear. The fetch-and-carry era is long gone."

"Hear, hear," Amy said.

"I do," Blue said, laughing, "all the time."

"Oh, yes," Amy said, "you're so picked on." She gave him a quick kiss. "Poor baby."

"Baby," Jana-John said. "Yes, that's what is missing from your training program, Bram. You and Glory need to have a baby."

Glory's eyes widened as she looked at Jana-John.

"Would you clarify that a bit, Mother?" Bram said.

"Certainly." Jana-John propped her elbows on the table and folded her hands beneath her chin. "I believe that prenuptial training should include the adjustments in life-style necessary when a wee one arrives."

"You're so wise, my lovely," Abe said, smiling warmly at his wife.

"Thank you, darling," she said, matching his smile.

No wonder Bram knew a great deal about the basics of loving, Glory thought. There was so much love in this home that it was filling the structure to overflowing. Of course, that still didn't guarantee that Bram would make a good husband.

Glory, pay attention, she told herself, in the next instant. Jana-John Bishop was chattering on about a *baby* needing to be added to the scenario. What on earth was Bram's mother thinking?

Jana-John got to her feet. "I'll be right back. It's easier to show you, than to try to explain. I have a baby in my studio." She hurried from the room.

"Mom had a baby?" Blue said. "Congratulations, Dad."

"Mmm," Abe said, nodding rather absently. "Back in history…"

Before Abe could continue, Jana-John returned, a bundle in a pink blanket held in one arm. She settled back onto her chair.

"I borrowed this baby from my friend, Mary Ann. She teaches a high school class called Living. She covers how to balance a checkbook, using store coupons, price comparing, budgeting and on and on. It's supposed to help prepare the students for the real world they'll enter when they graduate."

"That's a marvelous idea," Amy said.

"Isn't it?" Jana-John said. "They also have a section on parenting. They want the youngsters to think twice about starting families when they're hardly more than children themselves. That's where this baby comes in. I borrowed it from Mary Ann for my muse to absorb the vibes so I can paint a lovely picture for Tux and Nancy's baby."

"Uh-oh," Tux muttered.

"Didn't someone notice that their baby didn't show up for dinner?" Blue said.

Jana-John lifted the sleepers-clad baby from the blanket.

"This is a special doll," she said. "It's programmed to cry because it's hungry or wet or just needs to be held. See its little green belly button? If you don't respond quickly enough to its demands, a light goes on there on its tummy.

"Mary Ann said it has been a real eye-opener for her students who only think of babies as being cute, and have no concept of how much time and energy they take."

"I've heard about those dolls," Amy said. "I think they're a wonderful invention."

"Indeed," Abe said.

Jana-John wrapped the blanket back around the doll. "Here you are, Bram," she said, extending the bundle to him. "She's all ready to go home with you and be a part of your training program."

Bram took the doll and held it in two hands above his plate.

"Support her head," Jana-John said. "Your baby was just born, remember?"

"What am I supposed to do with it?" Bram said. "Glory? Help me out here, would you?"

"I can't," she said, laughing. "It's my turn to have an uninterrupted meal. We share taking care of her. Jana-John, thank you for thinking of this. It's fantastic. It will give me even more useful information to add to my course on prenuptial counseling."

"But..." Bram started.

A buzzing noise erupted from the doll.

"What's that?" Bram said, nearly dropping his cargo.

"The baby is crying," Jana-John said pleasantly. She took a small, plastic bottle from the pocket of her flowing caftan. "Here's a bottle of formula. If you don't feed her long enough, the alarm will start up again.

"The milky-looking liquid in the bottle actually slides down into a concealed cup above the nipple at a regulated pace. When you stand the bottle back up, it will refill for the next time. A device inside the baby will register the feeding, and determine when the infant has wet the diaper.

"If the problem is the need for a fresh diaper, you unsnap the one she's wearing, take it off, then put it back on as though you've changed her. Sometimes neither changing nor feeding will quiet her. In that case she'll have to be soothed by rocking or by carrying her. Isn't she sweet?"

"She's loud," Bram said.

"Oh, my," Glory said, then dissolved in a fit of laughter.

"Would you mind?" Bram said, frowning at her. "This is your baby, too, you know. You might consider helping me figure out what in the heck is the matter with her."

"Sorry." Glory attempted to produce a serious expression, but failed miserably. "Give her to me."

Bram handed over the doll as Glory scooted her chair back a bit to allow her to place the bundle on her lap. She unsnapped the cloth diaper, took it off, then put it back on. The buzzing noise stopped.

"Hooray for Mom," Nancy said, smiling.

"It was pure luck," Glory said. "I know absolutely nothing about babies."

"Guess what?" Blue said. "You and Bram are about to discover a whole lot of stuff about that little person."

"So tell me, darlings," Jana-John said. "What are you going to name your daughter?"

"Daughter?" Glory and Bram said in unison.

"Well, that's who she represents," Jana-John said.

"You're married and have a baby girl. She has to have a name."

Glory and Bram looked at each other.

"Do you have a favorite name picked out for a baby?" Bram said.

"I've never thought about it," Glory said. "What name do you like?"

"Well, I'm very partial to old-fashioned names, because that's what I want...an old-fashioned family, with a mother, father, a bunch of kids and a big house with a yard to play in. I want—" Bram shrugged "—what I had when I was a kid."

"Ohhh," Jana-John said, sniffling, "isn't that the sweetest thing you've ever heard? Abe, wasn't that lovely of Bram?"

"Indeed it was," Abe said. "However, I don't believe he understands what's involved in having three babies in diapers at the same time, the way we did."

Nancy splayed one hand on her still-flat stomach. "One at a time, please."

Glory and Bram continued to gaze directly into each other's eyes, oblivious to the chatter around them.

"You name her, Bram," Glory said.

"But she's *our* daughter. You should have a say in picking her name."

"Yes, all right. You suggest something and I'll give my opinion."

Bram nodded. "Emily. I'd like to name her Emily Glory Bishop."

"Oh, I..." Sudden and unexpected tears filled Glory's eyes. "That's very beautiful. Thank you for giving her my name."

"You're her mother. This business of only naming boys after their fathers, but not doing the same for mothers doesn't make sense. So, it's settled?"

Tux caught his mother's eye and mouthed the words "very settled."

Jana-John smiled at her oldest son, then leaned close to him. "They just don't realize it yet," she whispered.

"Well, people," Bram said, tearing his gaze from Glory's, "we hereby present Emily Glory Bishop."

"Bravo," Blue said.

"We're not giving you back the panda just because you've become an instant father, Bram," Tux said, smiling.

Bram glared at him.

"That doll really is marvelous," Amy said. "I'm going to present the idea of writing an article about it for the *Holler*. I think Gib McKinley will give me a green light. Spending twenty-four hours a day with the doll the way it's presently programmed *might* reduce the number of teenage pregnancies."

"Or increase the number of mature adults deciding to start a family they'd been convinced they didn't wish to have," Bram said.

Glory looked quickly at Bram.

Was Bram talking about her? she wondered. Or just making a casual observation? Well, it really didn't matter what he'd meant by his statement. She was excited about the high-tech doll and its possibilities for her prenuptial counseling course.

But she still held fast to the beliefs she'd had for many, many years.

She did not wish to marry.

She didn't want a husband.

She didn't want a baby.

Even if the cutie-pie's name was Emily Glory Bishop.

Nine

After consuming large bowls of ice cream, the Bishop family's traditional dessert, Bram announced that he and Glory had to be on their way.

"Aren't you forgetting someone?" Tux said.

"Oh, yes," Bram said, "and Emily. Cut me some slack, would you, Tux? You'll have nine months to get used to the idea of becoming a parent. Glory and I had about sixty seconds." He scooped the doll off Glory's lap and tucked it in the crook of one arm. "Ready to go, kid? Do you want to drive?"

Glory laughed as she got to her feet. "This is definitely going to be what is known as an experience." She frowned. "What are we going to do with Emily while we're both working tomorrow?"

"Back in history," Abe said, "the mother would keep the baby with her while she, say, worked in the fields. She'd have a large shawl tied around her neck to cradle the infant.''

"There you go, Glory," Bram said.

"Forget it," she said. "I'm not seeing my clients while I have a doll hanging from my neck. It wouldn't do much for their level of confidence in me.''

"I think it would be fair," Bram said, "to assume we checked out day-care facilities. We were very thorough, covered every detail to ensure that Emily receives proper attention.''

"Bram Bishop," Jana-John said, "Emily is a newborn baby. Surely you don't intend to put her in a day-care already.''

"You're right, Jana-John," Glory said. "We'll fix up a basket, and I'll take her to work with me. I can explain *that* to my clients. In fact, it will be a chance to promote the prenuptial counseling I'll be offering in the very near future. Who knows? They might tell their friends.''

"Fair enough," Bram said.

Farewells were exchanged, and Glory, Bram and Emily left the house.

"Do you suppose they know that newborns eat about every four hours?" Nancy said. "Whoever keeps her overnight is in for a surprise.''

Jana-John smiled. "Emily Glory Bishop will be fine, just fine. She has wonderful parents. Don't you agree, Abe?''

"I do, indeed," Abe said, wrapping one arm around her shoulders. "Did you know, my love, that back in history…''

* * *

"I'd like to stay at my house tonight," Glory said as they drove away from the senior Bishops' home. "I'm very tired, and I don't relish the mad dash in the morning if we've been in your apartment."

"No problem." Bram glanced at Glory and saw her holding the doll in her arms. "How's our girl?"

"Sleeping. Don't drive over the speed limit. If a police officer stops us and sees what I'm doing, I'll probably be carted away. This doll is soft, so cuddly. Do you think this is how a *real* newborn baby feels?"

"I imagine it is. The inventors of that thing seemed to go all out to make it authentic." Bram paused. "No, it's not a doll, not a thing. We have to get into the mind-set that it's Emily, our daughter, if we're going to do this right."

What was very, *very* right, Bram mused, was how Glory looked holding the baby, cradling it against her breasts. What a beautiful picture they made.

"I really like your family, Bram," Glory said, bringing him back to attention. "They're warm and friendly and made me feel comfortable and welcomed."

"They're good people." Bram chuckled. "By the way, those pictures my mother paints never get hung on a wall. She's really awful in the artist arena, but she sure has a great time painting those disasters. You probably noticed that no one asked to take the potato people painting home."

"You paid your parents a lovely compliment when you said you wanted a marriage, home, family, structured like theirs."

"It's true," he said, lifting one shoulder in a shrug.

"But a lot of men wouldn't have expressed those sentiments."

"A lot of men won't admit that they like quiche, either," Bram said, laughing. "Me? I just say whatever is on my mind—case in point our disastrous first meeting on the plane."

"Who could forget it?" Glory said, bursting into laughter.

Their mingled laughter danced through the air, creating a joyous sound that filled the vehicle.

Emily slept on.

There was, however, one thing that was most definitely on his mind that he could *not* say, Bram thought as he turned into Glory's driveway. He couldn't tell Glory that he loved her, was deeply, irrevocably and forever in love with her. No, he couldn't tell her yet. Not yet.

Inside the house Glory placed a throw pillow in the bottom of her wicker laundry basket. She added a fluffy towel and a soft, knitted lap robe, then settled Emily carefully in the makeshift bed, tucking the plastic bottle at the edge.

"There," she said. "Snug as a bug. Why don't you find room for the basket on the top of my dresser in the bedroom? Just move the things that are there to anywhere there's a spot. I'm going to take a shower and get ready for bed."

"Got it," Bram said, picking up the basket. "Come on, Emily." He started down the hall with Glory right behind him. "Do tiny babies dream?"

"I don't know."

"They might not because their subconscious wouldn't have anything to draw on. Think about it, Glory. Emily probably doesn't have the emotion of fear. Man, what a nice place to be. As a father, I wish I could keep it like that for her forever."

"Bram?" Glory said as they entered the bedroom. He stopped and turned to face her. "Yes?"

"When I was about six," she said quietly, "I had a best friend named Jenny. She told me that the twinkling stars in the sky at night were actually babies waiting to be born. I was very disappointed when I found out a couple of years later that it wasn't true."

Bram smiled at her warmly. "Maybe it *is* true."

Glory matched his gentle smile. "Maybe it is. What I wanted to tell you is that you're going to be a wonderful father. Your children will be very blessed to have you as their daddy."

"Thank you, Glory. That's a...a very nice thing for you to say. I appreciate it more than I can tell you."

They stood still in the quiet room, looking directly into each other's eyes. Bram held the wicker basket containing the doll that represented their daughter, Emily.

It was a special moment. A caring, sharing moment, of having turned yet another page in the book of understanding. It was a moment to be cherished and remembered.

Glory was the first to break the serene spell.

"Yes, well," she said, "I'd better get into the shower. I want to wash my hair, which is no small project. Maybe I should get it cut."

"No," Bram said quickly. "Your hair is beautiful, Glory. It would be a crime to cut it."

"A crime?" she said, smiling. She began to pull the pins free. "Like the one I was committing by not owning a pair of jeans while living in Houston?"

"Exactly."

"Goodness, Bram, you spend half your time just keeping me out of jail." She paused. "You must be getting tired of holding that basket. Why don't you find a spot for it on the dresser?"

A few minutes later Glory was standing under the warm spray of the water in the shower. She closed her eyes to savor the soothing cascade. Opening her eyes again, she began to shampoo her hair.

How strange life was, she thought, and how quickly it could change. It seemed like aeons ago that she'd been on that flight from Austin, returning to Houston. So much had happened since she'd found herself seated next to an enormous toy panda.

In what was actually only a handful of days, her existence had been turned upside down. She had a lover living under her roof, a man she called *husband*. And now? Heavenly days, she was acting out the role of mother to Emily, the baby girl supposedly created with that man.

On the clinical surface it was all sound, beneficial research that would hold her in good stead in her professional capacity in the future.

But deeper than that, on the emotional plane, Bram Bishop was becoming more special, more important to her with every passing hour.

Oh, Glory, please be careful, she mentally begged

herself. She couldn't lose command of those emotions and slip further and further under the mesmerizing spell of Bram's masculinity and of who he was as a person. She could *not* fall in love with Bram Bishop.

Glory frowned as she turned to allow the water to rinse the shampoo from her long hair.

Could she have been wrong about Bram's motives for wishing to embark upon his "husband boot camp"? He claimed he was taking the whole endeavor very seriously, and that certainly appeared to be true.

Well, be that as it may, she still believed that at least a part of his purpose was to achieve his goals of seducing her and reversing her stand on never wishing to marry.

He *hadn't* seduced her. The decision to become lovers had been mutually agreed upon by consenting adults.

As for his quest to change her mind on the issues of husband, home and babies, Bram was *not* going to declare himself the victor. Nothing—no one—could cause her to weaken in her resolve to remain free of potential heartache. She'd been the victim of her parents' marriage while a child. She would never agree to engage in it as a grown woman.

Never.

Glory stepped forward to wring the water from her hair, then turned off the faucets. The moment the noise of the water stilled, she heard Bram calling to her through the door.

"Glory? Now can you hear me with the water off?" he yelled. "I've been hollering forever out here."

"What is it?" She wrapped a towel around her body like a sarong.

"Emily is crying. Nothing I do will make her stop. I'm going nuts."

Glory laughed softly, then bent over and wrapped another towel around her hair. She flipped her head up, tucked in the corner of the towel turban-style then opened the door. The bedroom seemed cold compared to the steamy bathroom.

Bram stood before her, jiggling the blanket-clad doll. The buzzing noise emanating from the baby seemed to bounce off the walls, magnifying it tenfold.

"Good grief," Glory said. "She certainly has well-developed lungs."

"I changed and fed her. Sang to her. I bet...that's it. I scared the bejeebers out of her with my singing. I'm sorry, Emily, I won't do it again. Be quiet now. Okay?"

Emily continued to buzz at full volume.

"I guess this is one of those times when she needs to be held," Glory said. "She just wants to be soothed by human contact." She laughed. "Or whatever. I have no idea what her problem is, Bram. I know absolutely nothing about babies."

"Aren't women born with natural maternal instincts?"

Glory glared at him. "Were you born knowing how to change the oil in a car?"

"Oh. Good point. Well, do you have a suggestion, at least?"

"Are you certain you fed her long enough?" Glory

said, raising her voice to be heard above the shrill buzzing.

"I poked the bottle back into her mouth three more times."

Glory pressed one fingertip on her chin in a thoughtful gesture.

"She's not hungry," she said.

"No."

"Maybe the diaper came undone. Bring her over to the bed."

Bram crossed the room and placed the doll gently on the bed. Glory removed the diaper, then snapped it back in place. The buzzing buzzed on.

"The green light on her tummy hasn't been activated," Glory said. "That means you responded to her crying in a reasonable length of time."

"Hell, yes, I did. I nearly broke a leg getting to her when the alarm went off."

"Don't swear in front of Emily, Bram. We don't know how much a baby is capable of retaining at what age. You'd feel really crummy if her first words were *hell* and *damn*, instead of *mama* and *da-da*."

"I'll never swear again, I swear."

"Cute. Well, her diaper is all right. She just wants to be held for now."

"Go for it."

"I can't. I have to brush out my hair before it snarls."

"Well, I'm going to take a shower."

They frowned at each other.

"Couldn't you wait a few minutes for your shower," Glory said, "so I can tend to my hair?"

"Couldn't your hair wait long enough for me to take a shower?"

The frowns deepened to full-blown glares. Emily continued to buzz her displeasure.

"Damn it, Bram, why are you being so difficult?"

"Don't swear in front of my daughter!"

"*Your* daughter? She happens to be *our* daughter."

Glory picked up the baby, nestled her to the crook of her neck and began to walk around the small room.

"What happened to compromise?" Glory said. "Answer that one, Mr. Bishop."

"I did my part of a compromise. I took care of Emily while you showered. Now I'm simply asking the same of you. Are you willing to take your turn while *I* shower? No, of course not. You need to brush your hair first. Compromise? You should look up the definition in the dictionary, Mrs. Bishop."

The glares graduated to glowers.

Then Emily was suddenly quiet as a mouse. The buzzing noise stopped.

"Oh," Glory said, halting her trek.

"Hey," Bram said. He bent his knees to peer at Emily's face, then straightened again, smiling. "Nice work, Mom. You soothed her and took care of whatever was wrong."

Glory moved to the basket, laid the doll down, then tucked the blanket around her. She looked at Bram with a stricken expression.

"What's the matter?" he said.

Glory walked over to the bed and sank heavily onto the edge.

"We flunked parenthoodness, or whatever you want

to call it, Bram. We've only had that baby for an hour or so, and we've already been at each other's throats. Did you hear us? Listen to what we were saying to each other? Even more, think about the stress-filled atmosphere we created for the poor, helpless baby.''

Bram sat down next to her.

''You're right,'' he said. ''How did that happen?''

Glory threw up her hands. ''I don't know.'' She sniffled. ''I feel just awful about it.'' Tears filled her eyes. ''I'm a terrible mother. I subjected my child to the nightmare of hearing her parents quarreling. I can't believe I did that.'' Two tears slid down her pale cheeks.

Bram circled her shoulders with one arm and pulled her close to his chest.

''Take it easy,'' he said. ''So we blew it. It's not the end of the world. Emily isn't messed up for life, Glory. We're new at this parenting business, you know. I mean, hell...heck...we were still getting the hang of being married. The important thing is that we learn something from this. We really do have to compromise, to be more flexible. Right?''

Glory nodded, then sniffled again.

Bram shifted and removed the towel from her hair.

''Sit tight,'' he said.

He got to his feet, crossed the room to retrieve Glory's brush from the edge of the dresser, then returned to sit on the bed.

''Turn sideways,'' he said, ''and I'll brush the tangles from your hair.''

Glory did as she was told, and Bram slowly, gently, began to draw the brush through her heavy, wet hair.

After only a few slightly painful tugs, the brush began to glide smoothly through the silken tresses.

"Spun gold," Bram said quietly.

"That feels heavenly," Glory said. "It's so soothing, so relaxing. I don't know why it should be, when I think about it, but it is."

"Don't think. Just enjoy." Bram paused. "Before you turn off that always-busy mind of yours, though, I want to apologize for my behavior regarding Emily."

"I'm sorry for what I did, too, Bram. I really am." Glory smiled. "It's amazing how a tiny baby can turn two supposedly mature adults into overstressed, blithering idiots."

"No kidding. And Emily is just a doll. Imagine what an unpredictable *real* baby could do. Whew. People sure shouldn't jump into having a child because it sounds like fun, or whatever."

"Are you having second thoughts about becoming a father?"

"Oh, hey, no, not at all. I'm just getting a clearer picture of the fact that I'll need to be prepared to be right in there doing my share."

"Fantastic. I'm definitely going to purchase a doll like Emily for use in a section of the prenuptial training course."

"Mmm."

What he'd like to ask Glory, Bram thought, continuing to brush her hair, was if *she* was having any second thoughts about becoming a mother. Thoughts that were edging away from the negative toward the positive.

But to ask was to press her, and that was *not* a good idea. They needed more time with Emily. He'd watch and listen for any evidence that Glory's maternal instincts were rising to the fore.

Whoa, Bishop, he told himself. He was getting ahead of himself, *way* ahead. The subject he should be centering on was Glory's emotions for *him*, not a baby.

Were her feelings for him growing, becoming more intense? Was her protective wall weakening even a little? How was he to know? When should he tell Glory that he was in love with her?

Enough. He was going to take his own advice and not think anymore tonight. He was serving himself up a giant portion of unanswered questions that would cost him a night's sleep if he dwelt on them.

Bram blanked his mind and brushed Glory's hair, the sweeping motion becoming nearly hypnotizing. Her hair was almost completely dry, but he brushed on, watching the beautiful strands shimmer down her back.

Then slowly, but with ever-increasing impact, he became aware of more. Glory was naked beneath the towel tucked around her slender body. He inhaled her aroma of soap and flowers, savoring it. He saw the dewy hue of her skin that beckoned to him to kiss it, taste it.

Heat began to build, throb, low in his body. His hand holding the brush was not as steady as it had been, as his passion soared.

Glory closed her eyes to fully savor the sensations swirling within her as Bram worked his magic. She felt pampered and pretty, womanly and special.

Only a man who was very certain of his own masculinity would agree to perform the rather feminine task of brushing a tumble of hair. Bram Bishop was such a man.

She could feel the heat emanating from his massive body. That heat was weaving around her, into her, thrumming, pulsing, growing hotter now with every rhythmic stroke of the brush. Her skin was tingling, as well, the towel suddenly too heavy, intrusive, a barrier between her and Bram that she no longer wished to be there.

She wanted Bram. She wanted to make love with him through the hours of the night, hold fast to him, cherish the ecstasy their union brought to her time and again.

She would be Bram's wife, in every sense of the word, until the first vibrant colors of dawn streaked across the sky.

Bram set the brush on the nightstand, then lifted Glory's hair in his hands and watched it slide through his fingers.

"Unbelievable," he said, his voice slightly raspy. He leaned forward and kissed Glory's bare shoulder. "I know I keep telling you how beautiful your hair is, but it's true. It *is* beautiful. *You're* beautiful."

Glory moved off the bed and stood on legs that were far from steady. She looked directly into the depths of Bram's blue eyes, drew a breath for courage, then pulled the towel free and dropped it to the floor.

"I *feel* beautiful when you look at me, Bram," she said softly, "when I'm with you. That's a gift that you give to me, and I thank you for it. I want to make love with you now, I truly do."

With a groan of need Bram reached out and wrapped one arm around Glory's waist, urging her closer to stand between his legs. He buried his face in her breasts, which were partially covered by silken strands of her hair.

For a long, heart-stopping moment he held her, simply held her, gently, carefully, as though she was made of fragile, delicate china.

Glory rested one cheek on the top of Bram's head, savoring the texture of his thick hair and the unique aroma that was his alone. She felt cherished and special and safe.

She was filled with a contented, serene warmth at the same time the heat of desire was building to a fever pitch within her.

There was a childlike *rightness* about the sensation of being protected from harm's way by this big, strong but tender man. And there was the fire of womanly need that she welcomed, as well.

She felt complete in the embrace of Bram Bishop.

Slowly, reluctantly, Bram released her, ending the moment, yet anticipating what was yet to come. He stood and shed his clothes quickly, then they tumbled onto the bed.

And they made love.

Urgently, with a near roughness, they joined in a pounding rhythm, united, thundering in a matching tempo, soaring up and away, together.

The night was theirs. The night was wondrous as they reached for each other over and over, wanting more, giving, receiving, in perfect harmony.

At last they slept, sated, exhausted, heads resting on the same pillow.

As dawn's light crept across the bed in muted colors, Glory stirred and opened her eyes. She was quickly aware of the soreness of her body, yet savored it, along with the memories of the night shared with Bram.

She had shifted at some point to her own side of the bed, and turned her head to look at Bram.

Her breath caught, and her heart beat a wild tempo as she drank in the sight before her.

Bram was on his back, his lips slightly parted in deep sleep.

And there on his chest was Emily on her tummy, Bram's hand resting protectively on her blanket-clad bottom.

Tears filled Glory's eyes, and she pressed the fingertips of one hand to her lips to keep a sob from escaping. Shivering, she slipped off the bed as a cold wave of fear and despair swept through her.

She stared at Bram, unable to move, hardly able to breathe, seeing the man, seeing the father and the child he'd tended to as she, the mother, had slept.

And she knew.

Despite her vow, her determination, her commands issued to her heart, mind and soul, Bram had been too powerful, too all consuming.

Glory stood in the silent, dimly lighted room and knew she had broken the promise she'd made to the very essence of herself.

She had fallen in love with Bram Bishop.

Ten

She deserved an Academy Award, Glory thought wearily, as she sank onto the chair behind her desk at the office. The breezy, cheerful performance she'd produced while attempting to make her escape from the house and Bram had been Oscar-winning material.

It had seemed as though she had been floating outside of herself, detached, watching the bouncy, happy woman named Glory Carson acting out a role.

She, the observer, had been fighting frantically against stinging tears, as emotions tumbled through her mind in a never-ending maze. She'd registered stark panic, sorrow, a sense of failure, and had wanted to run as fast and as far as was possible.

Bram had appeared so massive in the small kitchen of her house, filling the room to overflowing, making it nearly impossible to breathe. His very presence was threatening, causing a tight fist to clutch her stomach.

She was in love with Bram, and that realization had created a whirlpool of emotion within her, spinning wildly, pulling her deeper and deeper into a place where she was terrified to go, refused to stay.

When Bram had encircled her with his strong arms and kissed her goodbye, she'd watched the other Glory respond to that kiss, then smile into the depths of Bram's beautiful blue eyes. The Glory she was had blanked her mind, forced herself to feel nothing as Bram's lips captured hers.

Arriving at the office with Emily in the wicker basket, Glory had explained the purpose of the intricate doll to Margot, who had been extremely impressed with the baby. To her own ears, Glory had sounded like a chirping bird, chattering a hundred miles an hour.

Alone at last, the wicker basket on top of a filing cabinet in the corner of the office, Glory propped her elbows on the desk, covered her face with her hands and willed herself not to burst into tears.

Dear heaven, she thought, what had she done? Even more, what was she going to do now? Today was Friday, leaving another whole week in the agreed-upon two weeks of marriage boot camp with Bram.

She couldn't do it, she just couldn't. The thought of living under the same roof with Bram for another week was paralyzing. He would know; he'd somehow discover her true feelings for him, the depth of her emotions. He'd see, sense, feel, her love for him.

What would Bram do…say? She'd be stripped bare,

vulnerable, open and exposed to heartache, because
that was what love, a committed relationship, then
marriage, ultimately produced.

Glory raised her head and stared into space.

But if Bram wasn't in love with her— Then what?
The image in her mind of him frowning, telling her
she'd messed up the training program by losing control of her emotions was so painful.

Oh, that didn't make sense. It was all so very confusing.

She didn't want Bram to be in love with her, to
complicate matters by declaring his love in return.

But what if he laughed, snapped his fingers and
said, "Gotcha, baby," as he crowed over accomplish-
ing his goals of getting her into bed, then lowering her
defenses and making her fall in love with him.

Dear God, what if Bram laughed as her heart was
shattering into a million pieces?

"No." Glory smacked the desktop with the palm of
one hand and got to her feet.

Bram had *not* achieved his goal. She had *not*
changed her views on never marrying. That she was
in love with him was a fact he would never know.
Somehow she had to keep her true feelings hidden
beneath a calm and cheerful facade.

But for another whole week?

"I can't," Glory whispered. "I just can't."

Pressing trembling fingertips to her temples, she
drew a steadying breath.

She had to get away from Bram Bishop. She had to
end the marriage charade as quickly as possible. She
had no choice but to take drastic steps to escape.

She was going to lie to Bram.

A buzzing noise sliced through the air, causing Glory to jerk from the sudden sound.

"Yes, I'm coming, Emily," she said, hearing the echo of tears in her voice. "Just for today, only today, Mommy's coming."

Shortly after noon, Bram slid into a booth in a small café and smiled at Tux.

"This is great," Bram said. "We haven't had lunch together in a long time."

"I had some business to tend to near the site your secretary said you were on today," Tux said, "so..." He shrugged and matched his brother's smile.

A waitress appeared, took their orders for hamburgers with double fries, then hurried away.

"Your Glory is a great gal," Tux said. "We all enjoyed meeting her, and the general consensus of the family was that she is a very special lady."

Bram nodded. "She *is* special, Tux. I... Well, I'm in love with her. I've finally found my forever love, I really have."

"It's obvious how you and Glory feel about each other, little brother," Tux said, chuckling. "You're walking neon signs, both of you. I'm happy for you, Bram."

Bram leaned forward. "Pardon me? Did you say 'feel about each other'?"

"Even Mom saw it, and our sweet mother is sometimes off on her rosy cloud. She told me, in so many words, that you and Glory hadn't quite figured out what was actually a done deal."

"You're saying that you believe that Glory is in love with me?"

"Yep."

Bram slouched back in the booth, flattening his hands on the table.

"Who do I have to pay to make that be true?" he said. "I know Glory cares for me but... Man, what I wouldn't give to be certain she loves me. I want to marry that woman, create a *real* baby Emily with Glory."

"Look, Bram, you know I was bothered from the beginning that your being close to Glory was based on a lie. Now you have another secret...the depth of your feelings for her. Don't you think the time has come to set the record straight about everything?"

"I don't know," Bram said, frowning. "Glory has a mind-set against marriage. If I declare my intentions too soon and pressure her, she's liable to cut and run. Telling her how I feel would be very risky."

"Love itself is very risky. There are no guarantees, Bram. The ultimate decision is yours, but I firmly believe that lies, including lies of omission, have no place in a relationship."

Bram nodded slowly. "You're right. Did you know that the number one cause of divorce in this country is lack of communication?"

"Then communicate with your lady, for Pete's sake. Clear the decks, get everything out in the open."

The waitress appeared and slid large plates in front of them.

"There you go, boys," she said. "Enjoy."

"Thank you," Tux said.

As the woman hustled away again, Bram stared down at his food.

"What's wrong?" Tux asked, picking up his hamburger. "We've eaten here before. They make a good burger."

"It's a tad tough to eat when you have a bowling ball in your stomach. I'm a wreck. I'm facing a helluva long afternoon until I can see Glory, sit her down and tell her how I feel."

"Eat up, because you're going to need all your strength. Remember that you'll be dealing with the most complicated creature on the face of the earth...a woman. We, as men, won't live long enough to understand them, Bram. All we can do is love them. But you know something? When that special woman loves you in return, it just doesn't get any better. Forever love, Bram. It's your turn."

"I hope you're right, Tux," Bram said quietly. "I *pray* you're right."

Early that evening Bram swore under his breath as he glanced at his watch after turning into Glory's street. He was later than usual in arriving at the house and hadn't telephoned Glory to say he was finally on his way.

According to his very-married brothers, the complexity of a woman made it next to impossible to always be certain what actions would be labeled a major mistake or merely inappropriate behavior on the part of an easy-to-understand male.

Would she declare war because he hadn't called to

say he was going to be late? He didn't know, but he was most definitely going to find out.

He'd left the work site and gone to his own apartment to shower and change into clean clothes. That had been important, Bram reasoned. This was not an ordinary "Honey, I'm home" night. He didn't want to arrive covered in cement dust when he was about to propose marriage to the only woman he had ever loved.

A trickle of nervous sweat ran down his back as he parked next to Glory's car in the driveway.

"I'm a wreck," he said aloud, an incredulous tone to his voice.

The bowling ball was still in his stomach and was now accompanied by a swarm of butterflies. His heart was beating so rapidly he was probably having another Glory-Carson-induced heart attack.

"Get a grip, Bishop."

He cleared his throat, smoothed the collar on the chocolate brown Western shirt he wore, then picked up the box of candy and the single red rose off the seat. Staring at the offerings, he frowned.

Were these gifts corny? he wondered. Well, if so, too bad. To him they were old-fashioned and romantic, just the way he wanted this whole scenario to be. Hell, he was even going to drop to one knee and hold Glory's hand when he asked her to be his wife.

His forever love.

"Don't swear in front of Emily," Bram muttered, getting out of the vehicle.

He glanced heavenward for a moment, then strode across the stepping stones to the porch. Seconds later he entered the living room and knew instantly that something was wrong. *Very* wrong.

Emily was on one of the chairs, precariously near the edge. There was no sign of the wicker basket. There was no sign of Glory.

Bram frowned as he stared at the doll, a feeling of foreboding washing over him like a dunk in a cold, unwelcoming stream of water. He placed the candy and rose next to Emily on the chair, then walked slowly down the hall to the bedroom.

Another chill swept through him as he stepped into the room.

Glory had a small suitcase open on the bed and was placing articles of clothing in it.

"Glory?" Bram said, his voice slightly raspy. "What's going on?"

Glory glanced up at him, no readable expression on her face, then resumed packing.

"Hello, Bram," she said, not looking at him. "I'm in a rush. I have a plane to catch."

Bram walked farther into the room to stand next to the bed. "Where are you going?"

"Chicago. My...my father is ill. He had...um... chest pains and is in the hospital. He'll be all right, just fine, but I really want to be there, see for myself."

"I'm sorry. That's rough. Your mother called you, I assume?"

"Yes. Yes, she phoned and—"

Glory stopped speaking, spun around and went to the dresser, then returned with several more items that she placed in the suitcase.

"Would you like me to go to Chicago with you?" Bram said.

Glory's head snapped up and she looked at Bram.

"No!" she said, nearly yelling. She took a quick breath and let it out slowly, the volume of her voice lower when she spoke again. "I mean, that really isn't necessary, but thank you for offering."

"Well, as your husband I'm prepared to stand by you in times of crises. You don't have to do this alone if you don't wish to. A husband should—"

"Bram, stop it." Glory backed up a step, then two, and wrapped her hands around her elbows. She lifted her chin and met Bram's troubled gaze. "You're not my husband. I'm not your wife."

Bram's frown deepened. "You know what I meant. We still have a week left in our original agreement." He paused. "Glory, why is Emily alone in the living room, appearing as though you just tossed her onto that chair out there?"

"The *doll* is on the chair so you can return it to your mother."

"Why? People face emergencies in their marriages. This is realistic. I mean, hey, I'm sorry, really sorry that your father is ill, but since that's the situation, we should adjust to it. If you're comfortable leaving the baby behind, then I need to make arrangements to tend to her while—"

"Stop!" Glory shook her head. "Please, just stop. We're not continuing with the boot camp, the training, the charade. We had a week and learned a great deal. But it's over, finished. Another week would simply be more of the same, and there's no point in that."

"Wait just a damn minute here," Bram said, raising one hand. "Just what exactly are you saying?"

"I believe I made myself clear."

"It's over, finished," Bram repeated, a muscle ticking in his jaw. "You're talking about more than just our training camp, aren't you? You're including *us* in your decision to cancel everything, right? Am I right, Glory? What we have together is over and finished, too. Is that the message I'm supposed to be getting?"

"It was a wonderful week, Bram," she said, her voice beginning to tremble. "I'll treasure the memories of all we shared, but we both knew it was temporary, our being together. It's just ending sooner than expected, that's all."

"I don't believe this," Bram said, shoving one hand through his hair. "It was a game to you, research with great sex thrown in as a bonus. None of it meant anything to you. *I* don't mean anything to you."

Yes, you do, Glory's mind screamed. *Oh, God, Bram, I love you.* She could hear the pain ringing in Bram's voice, could see it on his face and in the depths of his beautiful blue eyes. She was hurting him so much, so very much.

But she had no other choice.

She'd fallen in love with the magnificent man standing before her. That fact was so terrifying, so bone-chillingly frightening, that she couldn't deal with it and lacked the courage to embrace it.

She had to go, run, put distance between herself and Bram. She had to. And her heart was splintering into a million pieces.

"I care for and about you, Bram," she said, struggling against threatening tears. "I wouldn't have made love with you if I didn't. But you and I don't want the same things out of life. We have no future together, nothing to build on. Now, a week from now…what difference does it make?"

"Just a game," Bram said, his voice a hoarse whisper. "It was all just a game to you."

Glory felt a surge of anger within her and grabbed hold of it like a lifeline, clinging to it, forcing it to become bigger, stronger than the heartache that was beginning to consume her.

"You're accusing *me* of playing games?" she said. "Come on, Bram, how about a dose of honesty here? You were never really interested in husband boot camp. It was a ploy, a scam, to get me into bed and change my stand on never wishing to marry. How stupid do you think I am? *You* were playing a game, living a lie."

"It may have started out that way—"

"So you admit it?" Glory interrupted.

"Damn it, listen to me," he yelled. "Yes, okay, I invented the training plan to be near you. I wasn't upfront about my intentions, and my proposed need for learning how to be an appropriately behaved husband was a con. But my wanting to be close to you became very real, very quickly.

"I wasn't playing games, Glory, I was… Are you ready for this?" Bram laughed, the sound a rough, bitter-edged noise. "I was falling in love with you. Great, huh? Pretty funny, right? Even more, I believed you had very deep feelings for me. I hoped, prayed, I could break down that protective wall of yours."

"You...you love me?" Glory whispered. "Are in love with me?"

"Isn't that rich?" he said, volume still on high. "Hey, check out my spiffy clothes, the fact that I'm all scrubbed and rubbed, spit shined and pretty. Know why? Because I came *home* tonight with the intention of asking you to marry me, to be my wife. To be, Glory Carson, my forever love."

"No," she said, a sudden sob catching in her throat.

"I even brought candy and a red rose. Whoa, is that corny or what? I believed in us, Glory, in what we had, what we've shared, what we *did* have to build on. It was all there for us, I thought, if you'd only let go of the ghosts from your childhood. I believed that forever love would be stronger than those painful memories of yours." He shook his head. "What a joke? *I'm* a joke, a damn fool."

"No, no, you're not," Glory said, tears spilling onto her pale cheeks. "Oh, God, Bram, I'm sorry, I'm so sorry that I—" She shook her head as emotions closed her throat, making it impossible to speak.

"Goodbye, Glory." Bram's voice was low and flat. "Have a nice life, or whatever the proper phrase is for a situation like this one."

A shrill noise cut through the air.

"There's a good send-off," he said. "The baby is crying. Our daughter, Emily, needs her parents. But Emily isn't real, is she?"

He swept his gaze over the room. "None of this was real. It's really appropriate that I put the rose and candy on the same chair with the doll. None of them are even close to reality." He drew a shuddering breath. "So be it."

Bram spun around and strode from the room. A few moments later Glory heard the front door slam, cringing at the sound as though having been struck a physical blow.

She covered her face with her hands and wept, giving way to her sorrow. The buzzing noise finally reached her conscious mind and she stumbled down the hall, realizing that Bram hadn't taken the doll with him to return to his mother.

When she reached the living room, tears started anew as Glory saw the red rose and box of candy.

She sank to her knees next to the chair, scooped up the doll, held it tightly and began to rock, back and forth, back and forth.

"Mommy's here, Emily," she said, tears flowing down her face and along her neck. "Don't cry, sweetheart. Mommy's here."

Eleven

Glory sat on a cushioned lawn chair and stared up at the lovely old maple tree in her parents' backyard.

A soft smile touched her lips as memories floated across her mental vision. She saw herself on the tire swing her father had secured to a sturdy limb of the tall tree. She'd swung and swung, singing every song she'd learned that year in kindergarten, making up nonsensical words for those she'd forgotten.

In the next moment the carefree remembrances disappeared like a balloon pricked by a pin. She was once more dealing with the vivid memory of the last encounter with Bram. She spared herself nothing, forced herself to relive every painful detail, just as she had during the seemingly endless flight to Chicago.

She hadn't intended to actually make the trip to the Midwest. Her packing her suitcase, telling Bram her father was in the hospital, saying she had to rush to the airport were all lies. Lies born of her fear of having discovered she was in love with Bram Bishop.

She'd planned to hide out in her cottage over the weekend after sending Bram away, an actual journey to Chicago not necessary, nor affordable.

But following what had transpired between Bram and her, after seeing the pain she'd caused him and feeling her own, after hearing him declare his forever love for her, she couldn't bear to be in the little house alone with the memories.

So here she was twenty-four hours later, having run home to Mommy and Daddy like a frightened girl. She'd spent a long day attempting to behave as though nothing was wrong, pretending that her sudden and unexpected arrival was a result of being homesick. She was surprising her parents with a visit. Wasn't that nice, Mom and Dad?

Glory sighed.

She had no idea if her parents were fooled by her phony, cheerful facade, but they were delighted to see her, that much was obvious.

Glory had managed to avoid any in-depth discussion regarding her new life in Houston. Her practice was growing steadily, she'd told her folks, producing a big smile for them during the announcement, and she was slowly adapting to the vast difference in weather from what she was used to.

Guess what, parents mine? Glory thought dryly. I have just been told by the most magnificent man on the face of the earth that he is in love with me, wants to marry me and produce a slew of babies together.

Me? Oh, well, I love him, too. I love him beyond measure, beyond knowing what words to use to describe the depth and intensity of that love.

Why am I here instead of with the man of my heart? Oh, it's very simple. I'm terrified of loving my Bram, my beautiful Bram Bishop, because my childhood in this house where you still live is proof positive of what I don't want for myself, or for a child of mine.

Ghosts. That's what Bram calls my memories of growing up with you here, Mother and Father, and he's right. There are ghosts surrounding me here that are so powerful, dark and frightening.

The sound of the back door being opened brought Glory from her tormented thoughts. She looked up to see her mother walking toward her. Elsie Carson was in her early fifties, slightly on the plump side and had the same striking green eyes as her daughter.

No, Mom, Glory silently pleaded, just leave me alone. Please. I need to be alone to attempt to figure out how I can make tomorrow, and all the tomorrows after that matter…without Bram.

"Oh, isn't the breeze out here refreshing?" Elsie said, sinking onto a chair identical to Glory's. "The kitchen is a furnace, but it's worth the heat to be able to cook your favorite dinner. There's a pot roast surrounded by vegetables in the oven and an apple pie cooling on the counter."

"You didn't have to go to all that trouble, Mom," Glory said, smiling.

Elsie patted her daughter's knee. "It's no trouble if it's for you, Glory." She paused. "It's so wonderful to have you here, even if you do have to leave tomorrow, which is much too soon for me. Your surprise visit is like a birthday or Christmas gift.''

"Elsie!'' Glory's father yelled, poking his head out of the back door. He was tall and thin, except for the small bulge that edged over the belt of his trousers. "I have to go down to the hardware store to get a part for the lawn mower. The blasted thing ate a rock again.''

"Then go!'' Elsie hollered back. "But I won't hold supper for you, Joe. You and that Bert get to talking at the hardware store and you're gone for hours every time. When that pot roast is ready to be set on the table, Glory and I are going to eat it, with or without you.''

"Do I care?'' Joe said. "Your pot roast is as tasty as shoe leather. I *will* be back shortly, though, so I can spend more time with my girl, even if it means suffering through your rock hard roast to do it.''

"I'd like to see you cook a meal in this heat, Joseph Carson,'' Elsie said.

"It's a helluva lot easier than mowing a lawn, Elsie Carson.''

Glory was on her feet before she'd even realized she had moved.

"Stop it!'' she shouted. "You're fighting with each other again. No, correct that. You're *still* quarreling about all and everything.

"This ten-round bout is centered on pot roast and a trip to the hardware store? Well, why not? You two are pros who can create a disagreement over anything at the drop of a hat. That's understandable when you consider you've perfected the technique for decades.''

Glory swept one hand through the air.

"Carry on with it," she said, tears filling her eyes. "Who am I to interrupt? At this late date, why should you think of the ramifications your bickering might have on your child?

"Don't give another thought to the fact that I know, *I know,* you were planning on divorcing, then I arrived and spoiled the scheduled end of your marriage. Don't worry that I'll spend the night with the bed pillow over my head, or crying in the closet to keep from hearing your war, the way I did so many times when I was a little girl."

Two tears slid down Glory's cheeks.

"Why do you stay together?" she asked, shaking her head. "Hasn't enough pain been inflicted on every member of this family yet? What's the quota of heartache you're attempting to reach?"

A sob caught in Glory's throat and she sank back onto her chair, crying openly. There was no sound in the small yard except her weeping.

Joe Carson hurried from the house to where Glory sat, and Elsie rose to stand next to her husband. They exchanged shocked expressions, then turned to stare at their distraught daughter.

"Glory?" Joe said. "Baby? Don't cry, my sweet girl, please. There's nothing to shed tears over. Everything is fine. Glory?"

Glory dashed the tears from her pale cheeks, then looked up at her father, switched her gaze to her mother, then back to her dad.

"You call living like this fine, Dad?" she said.

"The constant fighting, the slamming of doors, the breaking of dishes? All that is just dandy?"

"Glory," her mother said, "your father and I have never considered divorcing. Never. Not before nor after you were born."

"I heard you scream about it," Glory said, anger now flashing in her green eyes. "I heard you telling Dad, yelling at him, that you would have divorced him if you hadn't gotten pregnant."

"I don't even remember saying that, because I didn't mean it!" Elsie said, splaying one hand on her heart. She sat down heavily onto her chair. "Dear God, Joe, what have we done? You and I have always yelled, thrown things, stomped out of the house when we were arguing. I had no idea that Glory—"

"Why didn't you speak up?" Joe said to his daughter. "All those years and you never once gave any indication you were upset. You were always such a quiet, poised little thing, a classy lady in a child's body. Oh, my darling Glory, why didn't you come to us?"

"And say what?" Glory said. "That I didn't approve of your constant quarreling and, therefore, it would have to stop? Dear heaven, Dad, I was the child and you and Mom were the adults. What was I supposed to do?"

"You cried...in your closet?" Elsie said, tears brimming in her own eyes.

Glory nodded, then stared at her hands now clutched tightly in her lap.

"I vowed early on," Glory said quietly, "that I would never marry, never bring a child into an environment that might result in the trauma I suffered in mine. I specialized in marriage counseling for the adults who come to me, but especially for the children who are the products and the victims of those turbulent relationships.''

''We, your very own parents, are the reason you've never married and had a family?'' Elsie said, shaking her head in despair. ''We were just being who we are, Glory. We yell, throw things around, clear the air, and that's that. We never knew that you were—''

''Glory,'' Joe said, ''listen to me, baby girl. Please listen to me. I love your mother. I have loved her from the moment I first saw her working behind the counter at the ice cream parlor more than thirty years ago.''

Joe drew a shuddering breath.

''Every night,'' he said, ''no matter how tired I might be, I pray to God that he'll take me first when the time comes, because I just don't see how I could make it in this big, lonely world without your mother. Oh, yes, we squabble and throw things…that's just how we are, who we are, but Glory, your mother is my life, my reason for being.''

''I…'' Glory started, then pressed trembling fingertips to her lips as fresh tears closed her throat.

''Oh, honey,'' Elsie said, ''I wish we could make all this up to you somehow. We never knew—you never said—that what you were hearing was causing you to cry. I'm sorry, so very sorry. Oh, Glory, please, please forgive us.''

''Let's give her some time alone, Elsie,'' Joe said, wrapping one arm around his wife's shoulders.

"Come on, you can go to the hardware store with me."

"Yes, yes, all right," Elsie said. "Oh, Glory, I'm so sorry, so sorry."

Glory watched her parents walk to the house, their images blurred by her tears. They appeared fuzzy, neither entirely clear, as though they'd almost meshed into one entity.

A nagging little voice began to nudge at the back of Glory's mind, refusing to be ignored. She tried in vain to push it away, wanting, needing, all her emotional energy to digest what she had just learned about her parents' love—true and forever love—for each other.

As a child, she now realized, she'd misunderstood what she was seeing and hearing. Because of her own lack of communication with her parents, the conclusions she'd drawn as a child had been carried into her adulthood, shaping her beliefs, the course of her entire existence.

The little voice gained volume, forcing her to listen to the words Bram had spoken.

You said your folks are still married. Why? Maybe they actually love each other. Maybe you're standing in harsh judgment of their kind of forever love.

Marriage isn't a chapter in a manual, Glory. It's real. Good times, bad, whispers of endearments when making love, and hollering your head off when you're pushed to the wall.

"Oh," she gasped. Glory stumbled to her feet and wrapped her hands around her elbows, oblivious to the tears streaking down her cheeks. She glanced quickly again in the direction her parents had gone, then looked the other way, staring into the space that represented to her the miles separating her and Bram.

How very wrong she had been for so many, many years, she thought miserably. It was as though she'd decided that because the shoes her parents had chosen to walk in were uncomfortable for *her*, then they had no right to wear them, either.

Maybe that was too simplistic an explanation for the high-and-mighty attitude she'd adopted early on in her life, but it made sense.

She was the one who should be apologizing to her parents, not the other way around. They had been true to themselves, knew who they were, what they had together. They were volatile, noisy, physical quarrelers and, Glory now knew, they loved each other with the same intensity.

Elsie and Joe Carson had forever love.

Glory Carson had nothing.

She had nothing but a future of empty days and long, lonely nights. She had lost the only man she'd ever—would ever—love because of her ghosts, fears and the lack of maturity to realize how very much in love her parents actually were.

Glory looked at the old maple tree that had stood firm, survived the rigors of time, the harsh winters and searing summers.

"I've learned so much during this trip," Glory said, speaking to the tree as though it was a person. "I'm changing, growing up at long last."

Fresh tears filled her eyes.

"Is it too late to tell Bram how sorry I am, how

wrong I was? Will he—can he—ever forgive me for the pain I've caused him?''

She moved closer and rested a tear-dampened cheek against the rough bark of the tree.

''Well, old friend,'' she whispered, ''there's only one way to find out.''

Early Monday afternoon Bram stood in front of a drafting table with his foreman by his elbow. They were in a small trailer they'd brought in to use as an office on the site of a twenty-story structure that Bishop Construction was building.

''See what I'm talking about?'' Bram said, tapping the blueprints on the table with a pencil. ''Come on, Henry, pay attention.''

''Cripe, Bram,'' Henry said, ''we covered that detail fifteen minutes ago. *You're* the one who has the problem concentrating. What did you do? Party all weekend? You look like a man who hasn't slept, and you've got the lousy mood to match.''

Bram straightened, dragged both hands down his face, then puffed out his cheeks as he exhaled a deep breath.

''I'm sorry, Henry,'' he said wearily. ''You're right...I'm bushed.'' Because I've paced the floor at night, haunted by the last time I was with Glory. Glory Carson is the woman I love, Henry. Glory Carson is the woman I've lost. ''You're all set here on these blueprints. I guess I'll head over to the shopping mall project and see how things are going.''

''Do those guys a favor, Bram, and catch a nap first.''

"Yeah, well..." Bram stopped speaking and frowned. "What's that noise? Oh, hell, it's whistles and catcalls. I've told the men not to do that when a woman walks by outside the boarding. Can't they follow a simple directive like that? I'm going out there and—"

"Whoa," Henry said, raising one hand. "I'll take care of it. In the frame of mind you're in, you're liable to deck one of our guys."

"Fine. Tell those jokers to put a cork in it."

Henry walked to the door and opened it. "Hell's fire, no wonder they're going nuts. The woman causing all the fuss isn't outside the fence, she's *inside*. Whew, what a looker, what a honey of a gal."

"Escort her out of here," Bram said gruffly. "And make it clear that next time, the cops will be the ones to end her little stroll among raging testosterone."

"It will be my pleasure to tend to that little lady," Henry said, chuckling. "She has strawberry blond hair that is a sight to see, falling down her back real pretty like. We also have very tight jeans to feast our eyes on, and a Western shirt that isn't hiding the news about what's underneath. She is... Uh-oh, somebody is in trouble. Deep trouble. Bram, she's carrying a baby."

Bram stiffened. "Long, strawberry blond hair? Tight jeans? Western shirt?" His eyes widened. "A baby? Baby! It couldn't be. Could it?"

He crossed the small expanse of the trailer in two long strides. "Move, Henry, I've got to see if—"

Bram was unable to finish the sentence. He felt as though he'd been punched in the gut, causing all the air to swoosh out of his lungs. His heart was racing with a tempo so wild he was certain that this time he really was having a Glory-Carson-induced heart attack.

Because, oh, yes, Glory was here.

Striding toward the trailer in tight jeans and a snug-fitting shirt, her chin lifted to a determined tilt, with that wondrous golden hair cascading down her back, Glory was most definitely here.

And in her arms was a pink blanket-clad bundle that he'd bet his last buck was Emily.

Glory stopped ten feet in front of the trailer.

"Bram Bishop," she yelled, "I want to talk to you!"

"To *you?*" Henry whispered to Bram. "I never figured that a savvy guy like you would get in this kind of trouble, Bram. Is that your kid that pretty gal is toting?"

Bram chuckled. "In a manner of speaking."

"Uh oh," Henry said, shaking his head. "I'm outta here." He slipped past Bram and hurried away from the trailer.

The smile that had formed on Bram's lips disappeared, and a frown knitted his brows.

Reality check, he told himself. Yes, it was wonderful to see Glory instead of just envisioning her in his mind. A part of him wanted to close the distance between them, take her into his arms and kiss her.

But another section of his being was raw, wounded, hurt to the quick by what had transpired between him and Glory the last time they'd been together.

Remember, Bishop. Remember that everything he and Glory had shared had been nothing more than a game to her, research to further her career. While he had been falling in love, she had been gathering clinical data. *Remember that.*

Bram stepped down from the trailer and walked forward slowly to stand in front of Glory.

"Hello, Bram," she said softly, looking directly into his blue eyes.

He nodded once. "Glory. I assume there's a reason for your stirring up my entire work crew?"

"I was afraid you wouldn't see me if I came to your apartment. I figured if I stood in the middle of one of your construction sites you'd acknowledge my presence."

"Oh, you're being acknowledged, all right," he said, glancing around. "You'd better come into the trailer before I have a riot on my hands."

Would her trembling legs carry her that far? Glory wondered. She could hardly believe she'd pulled this daring stunt, but here she was. And there was Bram, looking tired, grumpy and gorgeous. Oh, how she loved him.

Bram turned and Glory followed him into the trailer. She sank gratefully onto a metal folding chair and rested Emily on her knees. Bram slid one hip onto the edge of the small desk, then crossed his arms over his chest.

"All right, Glory," Bram said. "I acknowledged your presence, you've got my attention. What do you want?"

He was so cold and closed, Glory thought. Now *he* was the one with a protective wall around him. Would he listen to her? Really *hear* what she was saying?

Would Bram forgive her for the pain she'd caused him to suffer?

"Bram," she said, hoping her voice was steady, "there's so much I want to explain to you that I hardly know where to begin."

"Pick a spot," he said gruffly.

Glory lifted her chin another inch. "All right, I will." She paused and took a wobbly breath. "Iloveyou."

Bram leaned forward slightly. "Pardon me? You sound like you have marbles in your mouth."

"Oh, dear. Okay. I said, I...love...you." Glory nodded decisively. "Yes. There it is. I love you, Bram Bishop, with all my heart."

Bram stiffened and stared at her. "You do? You love me? Are in love with *me*? Bram Bishop?"

"Yes, but please listen to me. It's because of my having fallen in love with you that I ran away. I lied to you, Bram, and I ran like a frightened child."

"Go on," he said, hardly breathing.

"My father isn't ill and in the hospital. That was a bold-faced lie. I was so terrified of my feelings for you, I was desperately trying to put distance between us, run away from you.

"I didn't intend to really go to Chicago, but I was so unhappy after our last time together that I couldn't bear to be in my cottage all weekend alone without you. So I got on a plane and went to visit my parents."

"And the ghosts," Bram muttered.

"I heard that...and you're right, the ghosts. The stark and sorrowful memories of my childhood were all there waiting to pounce on me. And I thought those remembrances would reassure me that I did the only thing I could by sending you away.''

Glory fiddled with Emily's blanket for a moment, gathering courage to continue. She met Bram's intense gaze again.

''My parents started quarreling about a pot roast and a hardware store and…and I lost it. I screamed at them, asked them why they stayed together when all they did was fight, fight, fight. I told them how I used to cry in the closet when I was a child.''

Bram nodded, his eyes riveted on Glory's face.

''Oh, Bram, my parents were so upset. They had no idea I'd been so unhappy, because I'd never said a word about it. You were the one, Bram, who gave them the benefit of the doubt. Me, their only daughter, just stood in harsh judgment of their behavior for years and years.''

''I don't understand.''

''You told me that maybe hollering and throwing dishes around was simply how my parents dealt with their anger. You said it just might be possible that they actually loved each other, despite the yelling and screaming. And they *do* love each other. I know that now, saw it on their faces, heard them speak from their hearts.

''Bram, I went there as a frightened child. I returned as a woman who has grown and learned so much. I came home as a woman in love, no longer afraid to love, hoping, praying you'll forgive me for the pain I caused you. I do love you. And, Bram? It's forever love. I swear to you with all that I am that it's forever love.''

Bram lunged to his feet, whipped Emily from Glory's lap and set the doll on the desk, then gripped Glory's upper arms and raised her from the chair.

"And I love you," he said, his voice husky with emotion. "I've been one very lonely, miserable man since we parted. Ah, Glory, say you'll marry me. Please? We'll have a bunch of little Emilys. You're my life, my reason to get up in the morning, to breathe, laugh, to... You're my forever love, Glory Carson, until death parts us. Will you? Marry me? Be my wife?"

Tears filled Glory's eyes.

"Yes," she whispered, flinging her arms around Bram's neck. "Oh, yes."

Bram kissed her, and Glory returned the kiss in total abandon. The kiss was a promise, a commitment to forever love.

"Let's get out of here," Bram said when he finally lifted his head.

"Yes."

"Wait. Glory, you know that list of the ten most common reasons for divorce?"

"Yes."

"I've been keeping track. You've told me about nine of them. There's one left. What is it?"

"Oh, well, it's—"

Emily buzzed loudly, causing both Glory and Bram to jump in surprise as the shrill noise filled the small trailer.

"Goodness," Glory said, "she scared me to death. She's probably hungry. I tucked the bottle inside the blanket."

"Okay," Bram said, "but first tell me the tenth thing on the divorce list."

Glory smiled. "Boredom."

Bram's eyebrows shot up. "Boredom? Boredom, she says. Well, we can't have that."

He moved around the desk, opened the bottom drawer and removed a bullhorn.

"Bram, what—"

He grabbed her hand. "Come on."

Bram pulled Glory outside, the sound of Emily's displeasure following them. He pressed a button on the bullhorn and raised it to his mouth.

"Listen up, you guys," Bram boomed. "I want to introduce you to my future wife, the soon-to-be Mrs. Bram Bishop. This, gentlemen, is the woman I love. Say hello to Texas Glory!"

Wild, loud cheers and applause erupted from the construction crew. Bram wrapped one arm around Glory's waist, hauled her to him and kissed her. Hard hats were flung high into the air. Emily wailed on. Glory blushed a pretty pink.

"Are you bored?" Bram asked, grinning at her.

"Never," Glory said, laughing. "You're crazy, Bram Bishop."

"And you're wonderful."

"I love you," they said in unison.

They turned and waved to the exuberant audience, collected Emily, then with arms entwined, Glory and Bram went home.

Epilogue

"Oh, my stars, isn't that somethin'? Bram and Glory are so happy and so in love. Forever love is what they have, just like Tux and Nancy and Blue and Amy.

"Bram and Glory were married in the backyard of that nice new house of Nancy and Tux's. Bram built one of those gazebo things, sayin' it had special meanin' to him and Glory.

"Glory was a beautiful bride, with her hair tumblin' down her back and flowers weavin' through it. She wore a whispery dress that swirled like butterfly wings, and an old-fashioned big hat, like those Southern ladies used to wear.

"I sniffed my way through the weddin', of course, but so did lots of folks 'cause it was such a happy day.

"So, all the Bishop boys are married now, walkin' in sunshine. Nancy and Tux's baby will be the first of many those boys will be bringin' into this world, mark my words.

"Forever love. I surely do like the sound of that, don't you? I truly wish it for everyone who has a wish in their heart for it to be theirs.

"Little did I know as I was watchin' Glory and Bram bein' married, that there was love still hummin' in the air over some other folks, who didn't yet realize it was there.

"But that's another story for me, your ol' Granny Bee, to be tellin' you later on. You come to visit again real soon, you hear? I'll be waitin' right here in my rockin' chair, and I'll be mighty pleased to see you."

*   *   *   *   *

ATTENTION
ALL JOAN JOHNSTON FANS!

Silhouette Books is pleased to bring you two brand-new additions to the #1 bestselling Hawk's Way series—the novel you've all been waiting for and a short story....

> "Joan Johnston does contemporary westerns to perfection." —*Publishers Weekly*

Remember those Whitelaws of Texas from Joan Johnston's HAWK'S WAY series? Jewel Whitelaw is all grown up and is about to introduce Mac Macready to the wonders of passion! You see, Mac is a virgin...and it's going to be one long, hot summer....

HAWK'S WAY
THE VIRGIN GROOM
August 1997

And in November don't miss Rolleen Whitelaw's love story, *A HAWK'S WAY CHRISTMAS*, in **LONE STAR CHRISTMAS**, a fabulous new holiday keepsake collection by talented authors Joan Johnston and Diana Palmer. Their heroes are seductive, shameless and irresistible—and these Texans are experts in sneaking kisses under the mistletoe! So get ready for a sizzling holiday season....

Only from  Silhouette®

Take 4 bestselling love stories FREE

Plus get a FREE surprise gift!

FANTASTIC NEWS!

For all you devoted Diana Palmer fans
Silhouette Books is pleased to bring you
a brand-new novel and short story by one of the
top ten romance writers in America

"Nobody tops Diana Palmer...I love her stories."
—*New York Times* bestselling author
Jayne Ann Krentz

**Diana Palmer has written another thrilling desire.
Man of the Month Ramon Cortero was a talented
surgeon, existing only for his work—until the
night he saved nurse Noreen Kensington's life. But
their stormy past makes this romance a challenge!**

THE PATIENT NURSE
Silhouette Desire
October 1997

And in November Diana Palmer adds to the
Long, Tall Texans series with *CHRISTMAS COWBOY*, in
LONE STAR CHRISTMAS, a fabulous new holiday
keepsake collection by talented authors Diana Palmer
and Joan Johnston. Their heroes are seductive,
shameless and irresistible—and these Texans are
experts at sneaking kisses under the mistletoe! So get
ready for a sizzling holiday season....

Only from

CATHERINE LANIGAN

the bestselling author of
ROMANCING THE STONE* and *DANGEROUS LOVE

Searching—but (almost) never finding...

Susannah Parker and Michael West were meant for each
other. They just didn't know it—or each other—yet.

They knew that someday "the one" would come along and
their paths would finally cross. While they waited, they
pursued their careers, marriages and experienced passion
and heartbreak—always hoping to one day meet that
stranger they could recognize as a lover....

ELUSIVE *Love*

The search is over...August 1997
at your favorite retail outlet.

"Catherine Lanigan will make you cheer and cry."
—*Romantic Times*

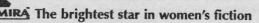

MIRA The brightest star in women's fiction

SILHOUETTE® *Desire* ®

15 YEARS OF GUARANTEED GOOD READING!

Desire has always brought you satisfying novels that let you escape into a world of endless possibilities— with heroines who are in control of their lives and heroes who bring them passionate romance beyond their wildest dreams.

When you pick up a Silhouette Desire, you can be confident that you won't be disappointed. Desire always has six fresh and exciting titles every month by your favorite authors— **Diana Palmer, Ann Major, Dixie Browning, Lass Small** and **BJ James,** just to name a few. Watch for extraspecial stories by these and other authors in **October, November and December 1997** as we celebrate Desire's 15th anniversary.

Indulge yourself with three months of top authors and fabulous reading...we even have a fantastic promotion waiting for you!

Pick up a Silhouette Desire... it's what women want today.

Available at your favorite retail outlet.